I0534009

MISS MANNERS FOR WAR CRIMINALS

a novella by

JACK SMITH

Serving House Books

Miss Manners for War Criminals

Copyright © 2017 Jack Smith

All rights reserved.

No part of this book may be used or reproduced in any manner whatsoever without the prior written permission of the copyright holder except for brief quotations in critical articles or reviews.

ISBN: 978-0-9977797-4-5

Cover art: Image from 123rf

Serving House Books logo by Barry Lereng Wilmont

Published by Serving House Books
Copenhagen, Denmark and Florham Park, NJ
www.servinghousebooks.com

Member of The Independent Book Publishers Association

Friends of Poets & Writers

First Serving House Books Edition 2017

Miss Manners is a work of exuberant genius. Jack Smith is fully in stride, from Dean's decent and muddled voice, and his gropings of conscience, to the intellectual bite of his anti-war theme, to the wonderfully distinct voices of his crowd of characters.

—**DeWitt Henry, author of** *The Marriage of Anna Maye Potts*, **and** *Safe Suicide*

Jack Smith has written a darkly comic novella, in equal measures poignant and surreal. The extended dialogue at his hellish family reunion reminds me of the opening scenes of *The Graduate,* with characters we may wish we didn't recognize from our own lives: the overbearing uncles, the soldier who, returned from the war, is on the verge of a spontaneous combustion, the graduate student who can't find a topic for his master's thesis. Hard drinks, a Hummer, young beauties with college degrees in comportment, the story is, in the end, a cry of anguish against our celebration of war and killing and all that is dark within us.

—**Barry Kitterman, author of** *From the San Joaquin* **and** *The Baker's Boy*

Miss Manners for War Criminals with caustic wit imagines a family reunion wherein a young host, in his existential struggle to find meaning, strives to use his intelligence among those who have clearly forfeited theirs. While reading I was strongly reminded of Eugene Ionesco's work. Like the esteemed playwright, Jack Smith excels in chafing the platitudinous while striking at the heart of the solitary anguish one experiences in what just might be a meaningless world.

—**Dennis Must, author of** *The World's Smallest Bible*; *Hush Now, Don't Explain*; **and** *Going Dark*

At a family reunion, Cousin Gere, a soldier back from war, goes out on a liquor run, suddenly loads his .45, and we know we're in for a wild party. With dialogue reminiscent of plays by Harold Pinter and Edward Albee, in this satirical novel the reunion-goers move from banalities and absurdities to speculations and debates on war and war crimes, and the justifications we dupe ourselves into. Meanwhile, Cousin Gere keeps reminding us that he was the one who was there. Dark, often darkly amusing, this novel is entertaining, thought-provoking, and relevant.

—**Robert Garner McBrearty, author of *The Western Lonesome Society* and *A Night at the Y***

The spirit of *Dr. Strangelove* is alive and well in this funny, trenchant, absurdist work of fiction from gifted satirist Jack Smith.

—**Christine Sneed, author of *Little Known Facts* and *The Virginity of Famous Men***

"The best proof for the wretchedness of existence is the proof that is derived from the contemplation of its glories."

Søren Kierkegaard, *Either/Or*

Books by Jack Smith

Co-authored with Eddie J. Girdner, *Killing Me Softly: Toxic Waste, Corporate Profit, and the Struggle for Environmental Justice*, Monthly Review Press, 2002.

Hog to Hog, Texas Review Press, 2008.

Write and Revise for Publication: A 6-Month Plan for Crafting an Exceptional Novel and Other Works of Fiction, Writer's Digest Books, 2013.

Icon, Serving House Books, 2014.

Being, Serving House Books, 2016.

Acknowledgments

Thanks especially to Walter Cummins, DeWitt Henry, Dennis Must, Penny Smith-Parris, and Mary Jane Smith for their help and encouragement on this novella.

To Mary Jane Smith

PART ONE
BLOOD RELATION

1

On the day of the family reunion, Dean left his apartment at ten in the morning and showed up at his mother's around eleven to a living room packed with people. Dean's mother escorted him around, making introductions. Near the door, there was Great Uncle George and his wife, Sally, on folding chairs. Sitting together, also on folding chairs, were his cousin Jennifer and her friend Ginger, both of them about his age. These two women immediately made Dean nervous because of their highly sensual looks, the first dark-haired, the second reddish-blond. But, he told himself, he must not be diverted. They were probably spoken for, and they were here only for a family reunion, not for picking up. But he found it difficult not to think of the latter, in spite of the fact that he already had a sultry girlfriend, Jill.

They came to Cousin Gere, decked out in his Marine uniform, with several rows of medals, just like Dean's dead father pictured in his Army outfit on the small round table near the door. Gere's parents, Uncle Rory and Aunt Winnie, relaxed nearby on the sofa, chattering to each other about something. Cousin Gere lounged in an overstuffed chair. "Your Cousin Gere is just back from the war, Dean."

He hadn't seen Gere since they were both small children. His mother wasn't the type to visit. But now here they were. "It's time we got everyone together," Dean's mother had said. But why?

Unable to think of anything much to say, Dean said, "When did you get back?"

"Week ago. You been in the service?"

"No."

"What do you do?"

"Working on my master's. On my thesis."

"Yeah? In what?"

"History."

"Yeah?"

"On war, actually," said Dean.

"Yeah? Which one?"

"Oh, I'm not sure yet. Maybe," said Dean, "all of them."

"That right?" Gere grimaced, and he looked away. He seemed to reflect on something, but Dean had no idea of what it might be. Gere's face grew slightly red, tinged with orange. Dean watched this until Gere suddenly turned and looked back at him.

Dean moved off.

Dean's mother said, "We've got plenty of things to drink. Plenty of snack food coming up. Plenty of everything, don't we, Dean?"

"Drinks, anyone?" he asked.

"Is Jill coming?" asked his mother.

"Maybe later," he said. He had asked her a couple of times but got only an evasive answer. Should he urge her to come? For one thing there wasn't much room to sit in this small apartment, with the one sofa, an overstuffed chair, several folding chairs—and possibly a kitchen chair or two if more guests arrived. He himself would probably have to take one of those chairs.

He repeated his call for drinks.

"Ah, yes, my yes!" spoke up Great Uncle George, waving a magazine, rising from his folding chair. It was the very magazine Dean had recently been reading at Jill's, one he'd toted over here the previous evening—*Know Your Brain*. Jill reviled it. She loathed philosophical determinism of any kind, and brain studies, she said, were the worst. Where was free will? They had excluded it altogether. "Animals," she yelled. "That's all we are to neuroscientists. Or machines." What did Great Uncle George think of it? But doubtless he hadn't much time to look too closely at it.

Great Uncle George was a large, beefy man with a huge bear head. He had a thick white beard and wore a white shirt with black trousers. "I could go for a stiff one about now—you, dear?" he said to Great Aunt Sally. But before he gave her a chance to answer, he went on: "More's the pity that most people don't dust off a stiff one now and then because it gets all the parts oiled up and in good running condition. Now . . . there are times when you don't *want* to do that—if for instance, you're about to make a road trip somewhere, but, and I've said this to Sal a thousand times, said it probably a half million times if I've said it once: you don't find a better way to relax your bones and get a new handle on your existence in this world than a stiff one. Now and then—I don't mean *all* the time. Just now and then, and you'll be the better man for it. I didn't say *woman*. Ha! What do you have, there, Dean—in stock?"

A talkative man. Dean searched his mind. They had soft drinks, some red and white wine, some beer, but nothing in the category, really, of "stiff." He hadn't laid anything in like that; in fact, his mother had said, "No liquor, Dean—I don't mean when you're in that aisle to purchase anything of that kind, but it's fine to purchase some wine. That makes it nice; it'll go well with the cheese and crackers. Hard liquor—it's too intoxicating, and we don't want that, do we? You see what I mean, don't you?" He had no particular interest in hard stuff himself, so he'd willingly laid in the red and white wine, about a dozen bottles of it, thinking they'd go pretty swiftly if a dozen people showed up, each consuming a glassful or two. But no hard liquor, unless his mother had some squirreled away from the past, which he greatly doubted. Did she?

He got his mother's attention. "Do we have anything in the stiff area?"

She looked at him, seeming to ponder this question. "No, honey, I don't think we do. But now you could certainly go out and get something on that order. If that's what's needed or desired."

Great Uncle George advanced toward them. "Well, and *I* would pay for it, Dean—Jean," he said looking at Dean's mother. "I would definitely spring for something a bit stiff about now. It being the time for something stiff, in good company, a bright sunshiny day outside, that blue sky just rinsed in sunshine, if you've happened to notice, as Sal and I did driving up that last leg this morning."

Great Aunt Sally combed back a cascade of blue-dyed hair and nodded limply. "So beautiful, so beautiful indeed. And so wonderful to be here, Jean." Was that a moan? A whine? Her voice sounded to Dean—what? Wistful? Yes, wistful. Yes, he would use that word to describe it. There was a sort of plaintive cry in it. He'd had a cat who whined, or winced, at discriminatory behavior, or at least he thought that was it. Intelligent, he thought. A cat worth something. At times he spotted sheer brilliance in that cat. Jill wasn't sure, but she allowed for the possibility. "Intelligent," said Dean. "I mean it."

"Okay," she said.

"He was free to whine," Dean had insisted.

"Maybe so," she said, but she didn't seem convinced.

"I'm so pleased that you *are* here," said Dean's mother to Great Aunt Sally.

"We're all pleased to be here, aren't we?" said Aunt Winnie.

"Yes, sir!" said Uncle Rory. "Most pleased."

"Well," shouted Great Uncle George, "what do you say, Dean, that you and I head on out to ye ol' boozerie?—I spotted one not far from here as I came in this morning—and grab us a couple of good fifths of spirits and return and make merry. What do you say?"

"Sure," said Dean. "Sure, that'd be fine."

"Yeah, yeah," said Cousin Gere, rising from the overstuffed chair. "I'll come with if you don't mind."

"Why no . . . well, but better ask Dean here. He'll probably be driving. Right, Dean?"

"I don't have a car," said Dean.

The man looked confused, anxious. He combed his white beard with a tentative finger. "How do you get around, son?"

Biking and on foot, mostly, he told him.

"Why?"

"It's a sort of protest," said Dean.

"Um. My! Well now, then we'll be taking my vehicle, and son," he motioned at Gere, "you are absolutely welcome to come along," said Great Uncle George. "I've got a nice big, gas-guzzling beast of a machine, and you are most assuredly invited to ride along and see what she'll do—and won't. Which won't be much!" He laughed. It was a loud one.

They headed for the door.

Cousin Gere paused at Dean's father's Army picture on the small oak table near the door. He studied it for a moment, ran a stubby finger over the four rows of medals, including the Purple Heart. He removed his finger. Was that a smudge? "Uncle Gene was a big army dude—hey? Officer and all." Dean looked to see if his mother was noticing. But no—she was talking to Uncle Rory.

"Yes," said Dean.

"Yeah. Big Army dude."

The three men left the apartment. "Don't be gone long!" shouted his mother. "Snacks are on pretty soon!"

"As long as it takes, right, men?" said Great Uncle George.

Gere said nothing. Dean said nothing.

They headed down the dusty stairs.

They got to the sidewalk, and walked on.

"Your mother is a great woman," said Great Uncle George, turning to Dean. "A great woman. To have all these guests in her small apartment, and half of them, I'll bet, she hasn't seen in twenty years. You know, we don't get around like we used to, families don't. When I was a little kid, people didn't move so far off, and we'd get dragged from one town to another, visiting relatives, sitting there in our white shirts, dark slacks, polished cordovans, and having to behave ourselves. Blood relation—that's what counts. Right? Doesn't it? You bet it does." They took up the entire sidewalk, and Dean found himself behind the two men, sort of in the middle position as they trudged along, Great Uncle George to his left, Cousin Gere to his right—two men he didn't know in the least, now heading off to get booze. And then what? He didn't drink booze much himself, only on occasion—mostly beer.

"My vehicle's parked right down the street, gents," said Great Uncle George. "Ever ridden in a Hummer?"

"Humvee," said Cousin Gere.

"I'll bet you have," said Great Uncle George. "I'll just bet." He laid a hand on Cousin Gere's shoulder, massaged it, then withdrew. "Well, this babe o'mine does her fair share of sluicing the juice, but what can I say? I treasure her. Wouldn't trade her for anything on this earth that I know of—unless it might be a bigger one! Ha!"

They came to the parking garage, about a block from Dean's

mother's apartment. "We're on Level Two, men," said Great Uncle George.

They took the elevator and stepped out on Level Two. "There she is, gents. Yellow like the bright sun above. Every time I wake up in the morning, grab my coffee and step outside in the energizing air of a splendid green morning in suburban Nash Town—I call her Pretty City—I see my Big Baby out there in the driveway, beckoning to me, like the kind of big toy I wanted as a child. Ready to romp. Like a cat on the prowl. And Sal and I'll take a little spin across town, and there you have it." He paused, cleared his throat. "You know, she's not doing so well, that wife of mine. Of course, you wouldn't know that. Hell, how *could* you know that?"

Great Uncle George aimed the remote at the Hummer. The lights flickered.

Yes, thought Dean. That distinctive whine. Plaintive.

"Cancer?" said Cousin Gere.

"No, no. Not cancer. No. You'd be likely to think it. At our ages, mine and Sal's, that's usually what sets in, doesn't it? That or heart disease, one."

They came to the Hummer. "Step in, boys. Step in."

They got in, Cousin Gere up front with Great Uncle George, and in the back, Dean, wondering where to sit. He decided on the left, right behind Great Uncle George.

"Not cancer. I'd think that too—worried about it half my life, when I wasn't worrying about something else. You know, you spend half your life worrying about things that never occur. I'm sure you've heard that one. Everyone's heard that if they've heard anything, and so I'm not telling you anything new at all." He looked at Cousin Gere as he started the Hummer. "I'll bet you know it to be true from experience. *Direct* experience. Hey?"

"Affirmative," said Cousin Gere. "It's the one you're not looking for that gets you. Damned straight."

"Ain't it the truth," said Great Uncle George. "Ain't it God's own truth? Well," and he began to back up the Hummer, with one arm stretched out toward Cousin Gere, and looked just momentarily at

Dean in the back, sitting to the far left, and funny how he gave him a wink, but he did, and then he backed up all the way, and then the Hummer lunged forward, and Great Uncle George gave it some gas, some noticeable pedal, and the Hummer shot out of the garage like a missile, and they burst onto the city street and growled down it fast, but smooth, with Great Uncle George suddenly having to brake as a Toyota pulled out of a parking place and almost hit him, on Cousin Gere's side.

"Hey, Missy! Watch out where the hell you're driving! Whew! Cell phone. That's what she was sporting with in that little Japanese job of hers, wasn't it?"

"Affirmative," said Cousin Gere. "Goddamned import!"

"Uh-huh," said George. "You know—about Sal. I hate to have to share this with you, boys, but Sal's not herself these days. So . . . if you happen to notice anything a bit strange or odd about her, it's because she's just strange or odd, whichever you prefer. They're both negative, but there you have it."

"Alzheimer's," said Gere.

"No—don't think. Could be, and I can see where you might think that's where I was going with that remark. But no, it's not that. Don't think . . . . It's something different. Dean, you're in school, Jean says. Maybe you've studied something like this."

Gere turned toward him. "I thought it was war, chief."

"It is."

"Get your war out of a book, huh?"

"More than one," said Dean. He tried a laugh.

"Jeez Louise," said Gere and turned back, shaking his head.

"Well," said Great Uncle George. "Well," and he shot by a slow-moving car, a VW Beetle, and pointed ahead. "Lovely little German thing—those VW bugs, vulnerable as hell, but I'm glad we're seeing more of them these days. Made them in Mexico for the longest while. Who knows what the hell they got paid an hour. Anyway, I used to like those little wagons, believe it or not, gents. Coming from a man who drives this big gas hog. Anyway, the liquor store's right up there. Right up there and bet you can see it."

"I see it," said Gere. "What about the wife?"

"Uh-huh. See, the thing is . . . uh, Dean . . . don't know if you've studied this or not, probably not, but anyway . . . anyway, here's what she's doing. It goes like this: You make a statement about the world today, whatever that statement might be. Maybe it's about the housing market slump in Pretty City, maybe it's about an outbreak of some dreadful disease, some strange disease you note on the Internet or wherever you see it, *National Geographic* maybe, some special on TV, or maybe you bring up the state of things in the war," and his right hand drifted to Cousin Gere's shoulder. "Well, gents, all I can say is . . . well, let me finish once we get done stocking up on some good stiff stuff," and Great Uncle George waited for a couple cars to go by in the oncoming two lanes of traffic, then made a hard left and shot across the two lanes into the liquor store lot, and landed with a thunderous thump.

They all bounced hard in the Hummer, Dean against the window.

"Hey! Fix your damn potholes! Son of a bitch!"

Great Uncle George eased into a parking place. It was all quiet in the Hummer for a moment or two. Then Great Uncle George said: "Well, now. Any preferences, men? Before we go in there? Anything on your list of faves in the hard booze category?"

"Right now," said Cousin Gere, "the higher the proof, the higher the regard."

"I'm with you on that one, buddy," said Great Uncle George. And he turned back to Dean, sitting far to the left in the back seat, about to open the door and step onto the asphalt lot. "What'll it be, Dean? What'll it be?"

"I have no preferences," said Dean. But he did think *beer. I could use a beer about now.*

"Hmmm. Well . . . an easy man to please, I see," said Great Uncle George. "That'll work two ways in this life. Get you what you want since you don't discriminate and get you what you don't want too. About half the time. Ha! Well, let's go, men."

They stepped onto the liquor store parking lot, and Dean, even though he didn't intend it, found himself once again behind Great

Uncle George to the left and Cousin Gere to the right. As though they were three men about to storm the place and demand what they wanted—or else. When that feeling became overpowering in him, he stepped back, and watched first Great Uncle George push open the door, then Cousin Gere follow him in, and Dean brought up the rear. Why was he even going in there? He had no intention of drinking any hard liquor. He was hoping they had enough beer, though—he thought they did. At a thing like this, a situation of this nature, he'd always found that beer made it go better. You drank up and you got your mind on other things. He wasn't much for reunions. Or didn't think he would be. He'd never been to one.

"Don't you want to get to know them?" asked his mother.

"*Will* I know them?" he asked.

She said nothing to that.

He idled in the liquor store and found himself to one side of the counter, thumbing through a rack of bumper stickers:

DRINK UP AND FORGET 'ER, BABE!

GOT DRINK?

DRINK-A-THON!

DRINKY, DRINKY, DRINKY!

Dean watched as Great Uncle George went about the store, grabbing bottles and stowing them in a red shopping cart. He soon arrived at the counter loaded down with a half dozen pints, a couple quarts, and three bottles of champagne. He set them, one by one, on the store counter. The liquor store clerk rang it all up and stuck the bottles in two paper sacks. "There you go," he said. "Must be a party somewhere, huh?"

"You bet there is," said Great Uncle George. "You bet. Just started!"

Cousin Gere was occupied with a rack of bumper stickers, thumbing through them. "Here's one, chief!" he shouted. "The fucking bastards!"

"What?" said Dean.

"Look at it. Just look at this motherfucker," said Gere, flashing it before him.

19

He looked.

DRINK, DON'T KILL!

Cousin Gere shook it, rattled it.

Dean looked closely. It was hard to focus with Gere's shaking. "Why that . . . isn't that . . .?"

"You think it's about drinking and driving? Yeah? That's what you think, ace? No—hell no. It's that same old goddamned liberal fucking media *We're-all-in-it-together* shit! I ain't about to kill my *brother* . . . No, way, Jose. Well, kiss my ass, motherfuckers!" Cousin Gere ripped it in two. Then he turned to the clerk behind the counter. "How much for this trashy piece of shit?"

"Why'd you do that?" said the clerk. His voice sounded pained.

"Because I don't like motherfucking bullshit out there that demoralizes men like me who have put it all on the line, buddy. *All* on the line. Every goddamned time we did what we did, we put it *all* on the line. For *you*. So you could be in this pansy-ass joint here selling us booze. That's what for."

Great Uncle George placed a hand on Gere's shoulder. "Hey, calm down there. Calm down there, comrade. We're in here to buy a bit of the sauce, not start a revolution."

"To hell with that," said Cousin Gere, jerking loose. "I need some ammo."

"Look," said the clerk. "I don't think it means that at all. It has to do with—"

"Don't give me that," yelled Cousin Gere, pounding his fist on the counter. "I *know* what it means. How much do I owe you?"

"Six bucks and fifty-three . . ."

"Yeah, yeah." Cousin Gere took out his wallet. He took out a card and slapped it on the counter. "Look, you give me some .45 ammo up there behind you. And about that bumper sticker, slick, if I were you, I'd pull every one of those goddamned things. I'm not coming back here myself—never."

"Sorry you feel that way," said the clerk.

"You're sorry. So sorry . . . well, you bet your ass I do, ace."

The clerk packaged up the .45 shells in a small sack, rang it up, and handed it to Gere.

"Hey," said Great Uncle George. "Hey, men, let's get back to the party and have a drink or two, and get back in the swing of things. What do you say?"

"Affirmative," said Cousin Gere. "Let's get the hell out of this goddamned place." He headed out with his small sack.

Dean followed them out, with Great Uncle George leading the way, carrying two large sacks of bottles, clinking against each other, the three bottles of champagne poking out of the top of one of the sacks. Dean wondered what it meant that Cousin Gere wasn't coming back to this liquor store. He wasn't from anywhere near this city—a state away, according to Dean's mother. Well, whatever . . . he wouldn't be seeing him after this thing today, so it mattered very little to him.

They backed up in the Hummer, and Great Uncle George said, "Now that pothole, gents, is not going to sink this ship o' mine if I have anything at all to say about it—not this time, not on my watch." And they crawled out of the parking lot, but still the Hummer descended a bit into the hole, and Dean could feel it, even with the good shocks. They shot out of the lot once they were on better pavement, and headed on back.

"You were saying about the wife," said Gere.

"Oh, indeed. Yes. Now, what I was saying about Sal, boys. Let me resume that, about this terrible, awful problem, which has done much to destroy my happiness of late. It's funny how you think you're sailing along just fine, and then a storm cloud like that. Okay . . . it's like this: If, as I say, there's *anything* of note happening on the news, anything that might seem threatening in the least little way, even though it doesn't threaten *her*—housing, for instance; we're not about to lose our housing since it's paid for, okay?— but just threatening somehow, and not just to people, but to any living creature, I'm serious now, anything that breathes and has blood flowing through its veins . . . no, I take it back . . . even the Grand Canyon, my god, yes! . . . even some river—pollution, you know, well, hell . . . she'll begin to tear up. You know, cry. Not start

21

sobbing necessarily, but close to it. And sometimes she *will* sob, give it a good rinsing out. So I've pretty well shut the TV off—news anyway. Get my news on the Internet. But how can you explain it? I don't think I *can* explain it. Depression? Some mental condition? Something deteriorating there? Had her at a couple shrinks, ones she'd allow me to take her to, but hell, they don't know a thing. Not a single thing. Got her some pills, though, and I've packed a couple vials with me." He patted his jacket. "Hard to get her to take the little bastards, but you know . . . I carry them just in case—"

"Post-traumatic stress," said Gere. He removed a pack of cigarettes. "Mind?" He turned toward Dean. "You, hoss?"

"Well, it's not exactly my—"

"Yeah, yeah. George?"

Silence. Then Great Uncle George's voice kind of shaky, scratchy: "Sorry, Gere, buddy, but I *do*. I don't want my Big Baby stunk up with smoke. Is that okay?"

He smirked and shot around a truck. He whipped back in, within inches of a small green car.

"Yeah, yeah." Gere deposited his pack of Marlboros. "So no dice on the shrinks, hey?"

"No. Got them all puzzled."

"Yeah? Depression, hoss. I've seen it."

"Well, maybe," said Great Uncle George. "But from what? Everything's been just wonderful for us. Retired now for five years in the Pretty City. No longer out busting my ass selling, no longer cussing a blue streak over this, that, or the other, living pretty damned well with one hell of a nice pension, stock options, house flat-out paid for, grandkids growing up, kids doing pretty well up there in the Last Great Frontier—so I just can't imagine. Can't even begin to put my finger on what's going on there. It started right after I got retirement, though, you know that? Maybe she's just unhappy as hell that I'm home all the time! You figure it's that, boys? Ha!" But he was looking at Gere.

"Fucked up, George. Affirm on that. Fucked up real bad."

"Well, I wish . . . hell, I wish you wouldn't put it that way, Gere."

"Yeah? What way would you put it?"

Suddenly: "Gere! Hey!"

Dean looked.

There it was: shiny black metal—a pistol.

"Whew!" said Great Uncle George. "Hey, what the—"

"Fuck? Just loading her up, hoss. Gere plunged his hand in his small sack. "Got my ammo here, and loading her up, George. That's all there is to it. No sweat—hey?"

"But out here—in broad daylight—in public?"

"Have her done here in a minute." Cousin Gere poked in brass bullets, holding up the pistol, turning it so that the sun blasted it brilliant white. Then he gave it a quick kiss on the barrel. "No sooner said than done, eh?" He sat forward. "No reason to have a piece if it's not got anything in it. Is there?"

Great Uncle George sighed.

"What's that about?" said Gere. He sounded mean, nasty.

"No—guess you're right there, Gere. Good point," said Great Uncle George. "Good point!"

"Back in the pocket now," said Gere. "In case you got a big prob—protection, see?"

"Oh, hell," said Great Uncle George, "I guess that comes naturally to you, huh, pal?"

"You damned straight it does."

Great Uncle George whipped past another slow-moving vehicle, olive-colored. "Not a bad car there, like that color. Economy job, but then we're all going to have to move into that category pretty soon, aren't we—me most of all. Damned global warming, huh? Ha! Look, Gere, we saw two, three of those neurologist types, and they don't have the slightest idea on it. Sure, they did the scans, the MRIs, the MRAs, the CATS, the this, the that, the what have you, but not a one of them turns up anything. She just leaks the tears, starts the faucet—go figure. Well, what *is* that about? We're talking tear ducts, tears from the lachrymal gland, or whatever, and then something's causing that to happen—but *what*? How can you ever know exactly what that thing is which is causing that to happen?

You get down to the wires, the circuits, but you think the answer's in the circuitry? Probably is, but how are you ever going to find it?" Great Uncle George let out a whoop. "Nice car there too—that one," he said, as they passed a Cadillac Escalade. "What Tony Soprano drove, wasn't it? I could go for one of those, but probably not in this lifetime, huh? Can't afford that *and* this, now can I? Huh? Ha!"

"Negative," said Cousin Gere. "Hey, hoss, I had a captain who looked a lot like Tony Soprano. Talked like him too. Ran his outfit like him. You never knew if this guy would take you off at the knees or give you a big kiss on both cheeks—if you get my drift."

"I do," said Great Uncle George. "I sure do, Gere. Had a merchandising manager I had to deal with, and I got to thinking of this guy as Tony Soprano. I used to tell Sal that I could do without the sales in that place just to get rid of that bastard. Spooky. Was in the gun market, and I do love guns, got a whole houseful, but I swear, Gere, there was something wrong in the brain department in that guy. You know it when you see it. You know—quacks like a duck, right?"

"Affirm," said Cousin Gere.

"Been thinking," said Great Uncle George, "that a woman like Sal must have something in her past—if we're not talking about something that happened, as you say, Gere, of recent date to trigger a thing like that. Or maybe she's just down. You know. Old age? You reckon?"

No response.

Great Uncle George cleared his throat. "You think it is old age—fear of death, maybe? Does strange things to us, you know, old pal."

"How the fuck would I know?" said Gere. He was looking out the window, and seemed to be lost in thought.

"Don't think it's her past exactly. She's a woman with a pretty ordinary past, like mine. We grew up in the best of times, see, policing the planet, space age—you name it. The whole enchilada. Sure we were scared. Hell, yes, we were scared. The whole goddamned world could blow up any minute, but we had it covered—or hoped we did. Anyway, rock bottom? We knew we were *right*, you bet

24

we did, and we were happy as hell about it too. Couldn't tell us we shouldn't be. And had a lot of new household gadgets to keep us smiling—TVs, clothes washers, toasters, mixers, you name it. I don't see that these days," said Great Uncle George. "I don't see that—hell, that kind of optimism. A lot of gloom out there."

"That right, chief?" said Gere, whipping around. "You don't think we're right—that what you're saying?"

"Oh, no, hell yes, we're right!" said Great Uncle George. "We're right as rain, but I just don't see that—that uplifting feeling anymore."

"That's because of the goddamned, lily-livered son-of-a-bitches!" shouted Cousin Gere. "The goddamned fucking liberal media! A fucking conspiracy!" And he slammed his hand down.

It made a real wham. Dean jerked.

"Whoa! Watch the merchandise there," said Great Uncle George. He shot into the parking building just then. "Watch ye old merchandise, buddy boy—if you would, please."

"Yeah," said Gere. "Sorry."

"Well, hell, it's okay," said George.

They parked on Level Two, as before, in almost the same exact spot.

Great Uncle George sat there a few moments. "I always like to find the place where I was before. Otherwise, ever spent a few hours looking for your machine? No fun, is it? And maybe it's just my age showing, but—"

"Yeah, sure," said Cousin Gere. "Lost my Humvee a couple times. Due to chaos—okay? I'm talking *chaos*. Get my drift?"

"Oh I do, I do indeed," said Great Uncle George. "Spent some of my own time in places like that, but don't mention any such things to the group assembled in Jean's apartment, please, because, as I've said about Sal—"

"Real geyser, huh?" said Cousin Gere. "Lips sealed, George."

"Tighter than a drum, as they say," said Great Uncle George. He stepped out of the Hummer onto the parking lot pavement, and Dean did too, and so did Cousin Gere, and Great Uncle George pointed his remote, and there went the clicking sound and the flashing of lights. "Oh, we'll see her cry, that's a foregone conclusion, boys, but over what?—well, that's up for grabs. It won't be because the food's not to her liking—Dean—or the drinks, or anything of that nature. Somebody'll touch on one of the harsher things going on in the world, and it won't have to be death-related, not directly, but to Sal, see, it *will* be—see, there's the kicker right there. Everything, I swear is death-related to her. And maybe that's it, just a big fear of death, at her age, see—sixty-nine, you know. When the Reaper starts peering around the corners at you, maybe that's when the wiring goes bad. Maybe you see into it all, things you didn't see before. Reckon?"

No response.

They walked on, with Dean finding himself, once again, behind the other two, in the middle, and he swore when they got out on the sidewalk, he'd take either the left or the right position—abreast of them.

"You take your little kid, six or seven, they don't see much. Do they? They don't see much of anything at all, other than what's going to bring immediate gratification. Move a couple notches or so, and your kid starts asking questions, about whether this or that will *remain*—will it last, will it run out? Will it be worth it? Get to your age, Gere or Dean," he said, turning to give Dean a quick smile, "you really probe it all—and if you didn't, you'd be the biggest sucker that ever lived. Get to be my age, you get cynical—you've seen it. Seen it all and more. It comes in different packages, but you can spot it all the same. So Sal? Maybe she's just downright depressed. Feels like she's been sold a bill of goods, maybe, and she's about to put one foot into the grave—and this is it? This is all it *was*—for your biblical three score and ten? That's all the damn thing added up to?" Great Uncle George let out a jittery laugh. "Naw, though, I don't think that's it. I really don't. She likes our life too much down there in the Pretty City. When she's smiling, when there's no—you know, trouble. So I don't know *what* the hell it is."

A ways down the sidewalk, Dean quickly repositioned himself, merging to the left of Great Uncle George on the building side.

"Fear," said Gere.

"Hmm? What's that?"

"Fear. She's got the fear in her. I've seen it. Seen it plenty."

"Death, then. Think it's that—do you?"

"Fear," said Gere.

"Hmmm," said Great Uncle George. "But fear of what, bud? What's she got to fear?"

"Hell, how the fuck would I know?"

"Sure. Sure. But no break-ins in our neighborhood, no robberies at the local convenience stores, no school shootings. Even got a neighborhood watch thing going. We're squeaky clean down there, Gere. So what the hell?"

No response.

"Well, hell," said Great Uncle George. And then they trudged on to the apartment.

2

"Well, you're back," said his mother. She was smiling big at them. Was she trying too hard to do it? Dean thought she looked too thin. And that gray in her hair.

"Jean, we're sorry it took so long," said Great Uncle George. "But it's that walk-a-thon to and from the parking building, the traffic and so forth . . . and then time to pick out the right hard or stiff stuff—you know." He held up the two sacks of bottles before those assembled in the small living room. "You'd think they could package it up a little more interestingly. In paper sacks like this. Shame, *shame*." He laughed.

"George, just put it in the kitchen, please," said Great Aunt Sally. In a plaintive voice? Yes, wasn't it? She was now sitting on the sofa with Uncle Rory and Aunt Winnie. Perhaps she was okay. Perhaps they would aid and soothe the poor old woman, though she didn't look particularly anguished about anything right now. He'd be sure to watch closely, though.

"In a minute here," said Great Uncle George, giving her a quick look.

"I'll get 'em," shouted Uncle Rory and he went for the sacks of bottles and walked them to the kitchen. Then he pivoted and returned and sat back down next to his wife.

"You're a gentleman, Rory," spoke up Jennifer.

"Maybe I'm just thirsty," Uncle Rory shot back.

"My husband's a real guzzler," said Aunt Winnie.

"My husband is too," said Ginger. "Especially when he's on the hunt." She let out a guffaw. "He drinks more than he shoots."

"I guess the deer don't mind," said Jennifer.

A man Dean didn't recognize said, "Well, if your husband misses—I suppose you're right."

"You hunt?" said Gere. He thumped Dean's arm.

"No," said Dean, moving off.

"Me neither," said Gere. "You think I got time for that?"

"No. Guess not."

28

Dean's mother jumped in. "Oh my gosh, I almost forgot—oh, please do forgive, but Uncle George, please meet—"

"Tom," said the tall, slender man who now rose from a folding chair. "Tom, Jean's uncle, from way out West. They all call me Tommy—affectionately, of course." He gave a sly wink. "And you're—"

"George. From down in Nash Town. We call it the Pretty City. And my wife there, the one who just sent the liquor to the kitchen . . . well, that's Sally over there."

"Well, George, we've already met," said Great Aunt Sally. "Of course, Jean introduced her uncle to me. Of course she would."

"Oh, of course," said Great Uncle George. "Of course. While I was out there buying the fuel for the fire, naturally Jean would introduce everyone. Naturally. Now here's who *I* am," said Great Uncle George. "I'm Gene's uncle . . . whoops, well, Gene spelled with a 'G'—not Jean here, our hostess. I'm embarrassed, damn, having just said that— surely you'd *know* that." He stood there, with his hand still shaking Great Uncle Tommy's hand. "See, to make matters worse, or more confusing, Gene, her departed husband—his picture's over there . . . in his Army uniform there, well, I suppose you know that too! . . . well, anyway, Gene's father was named Gene also, I'm George, his brother—two brothers in the family starting with the letter 'G,' then Gene himself, my departed nephew—it's all very confusing, isn't it? Then Jean, his wife, same sound, different letter. But them's the facts. I'd sure hate to be doing the genealogy—"

"A puzzle," said Great Uncle Tommy, smiling brightly. "I'm Jean's uncle on her father's side." Dean thought him quite remarkable: 6' 2" probably, slim, well-built, with a clean shaven face, and immaculately combed, oily black hair. He could be a general or a politician.

"Genealogy," said Great Uncle George. "Don't think I'd be much good at it. But blood's thicker than water, and you can see why people get into it. Makes a difference if you've got a family. If you don't have that, what have you got? The rest of the world can go suck eggs, right? But your family—well, that's a different matter, now isn't it?"

29

"Blow them the fuck to hell!" said Gere, with a snarling laugh.

Great Uncle Tommy stepped back. "Whew! My heavens! Now you're . . ."

"Gere Packall."

"Oh, of course," said Great Uncle Tommy, shaking hands with Gere. "Of course. And thank you for your service, sir."

"Don't call me sir," said Gere.

"No, no," said Great Uncle Tommy. He shook his head. Then he quickly turned to Great Uncle George. "You were saying—"

"Family, Tommy. Blood."

"George, you're right. You can't depend on the general man out there. No matter what you hear, everyone out there is just a stranger in comparison, other than maybe a handful of close friends. And you get to our age, you see that, don't you? Now, I think we *did* meet, didn't we, once upon a time . . ."

"Let me think back," said Great Uncle George. "When would it have been?"

"Weren't you there at the reunion out West—oh, twenty years ago?"

"No—no, I wasn't."

"Well, maybe I'm confusing you with someone else."

"Probably are," said Great Uncle George.

"But at least we meet now," said Great Uncle Tommy. "That's what counts. Gene's uncle, huh?" He turned to the whole group assembled. "There was an honorable man—that man there." He pointed at the picture.

They all looked.

"A handsome man," said Jennifer.

"A real hero," said Ginger.

"Gave his life," said Great Uncle George.

"So we could live," said Uncle Rory.

"Oh, dear," said Aunt Winnie. "Oh, dear!"

Great Aunt Sally. She was looking at the picture too. Wasn't she? A slight tremble in her lips. Slight, but noticeable.

An officer, Dean thought: his father an officer with all those medals. They seemed to glint in the sun casting a crooked ray through the Venetian blinds.

That picture, Dean thought: it had inspired him, in a way—a very distinct way—to choose war as his thesis topic. Over the years, his mother had filled his ears with his father's impeccable Army record. His deeds of honor and glory. But then dead. How? She wouldn't tell him. Dean was somehow stimulated: he had filled almost an entire spiral notebook with counts of war dead over many a war and his own reflections on them: the mutilation of bodies, the snuffing out. Carnage. Blood, gore. It seemed a good start. But where to go with it? He couldn't quite imagine. His thesis director, Harry, said, "Sounds a bit platitudinous, Dean."

He stared at Harry, unsure. He fidgeted. Something must come of this.

He tended to rant. When he got in certain moods, anyway.

"Well, whatever you do, don't bring that up at the reunion!" his mother had warned.

"No, no," he assured her.

"I mean it now. What would they think? Your father a decorated man, and you talking like that. Did he die utterly in vain?"

"You need not worry," he said.

"Just see that you don't," she said.

Dean continued to watch Great Aunt Sally's reaction. She seemed to be preoccupied with that photo.

"An honorable man indeed," said Great Uncle George. "Brave. To the end." And he turned to look at Dean's mother, who had her hand against her mouth. "But tragic. Tragic indeed. But let's don't take on about that now. Let's all celebrate the life we do have—and Jean's with it."

"That's exactly right," said Great Uncle Tommy. "That's the spirit." His voice was a mellow baritone. There was authority in it, Dean thought. Something like The Last Word. You wouldn't be likely to question anything Tom or Tommy said.

"Well," said Great Uncle George, "I think we've got plenty of joy juice now—" He headed for the kitchen.

31

"Are you going to start that right now?" asked Great Aunt Sally.

He turned to look at her and came to a stop. "No. Not if you don't want me to, Sal."

"Oh, it will be just fine," said Dean's mother. "A drink or two won't disturb the world. Would anyone want wine or anything, beer—or one of George's hard drinks? Or tea or coffee or soft beverages? Or bottled water? We have bottled water, don't we, Dean? Plenty of it, don't we, dear?"

"Plenty," said Dean. "And snack crackers."

"Yes, and that's coming. With cheese. But don't spoil your supper. Save plenty of room for that," said his mother. "But do eat up—we've got lots."

"We've got a little surprise in regard to that supper business, don't we, Jean?" spoke up Great Uncle Tommy.

"Well, *you* do," said Dean's mother and blushed.

"Myself," said Cousin Gere, "I'd go for a Beam."

"Take a Beam myself," said his father, Uncle Rory. "You, dear?" he said to Aunt Winnie.

"I don't care—just whatever," she said.

"Well, that makes it more difficult," said Uncle Rory, "instead of easier. Just say beer, Beam, Coke—give them something to work with, honey."

"Coke," she said. "That'd do me."

"You want something in it?" asked Uncle Rory.

"Dad," said Cousin Gere. "She's never spiked her Cokes. Hell, man."

"Well," laughed Uncle Rory. "How would *I* know?"

"Rory," said Dean's mother, laughing, "surely, you'd know what your wife drinks. Whether she's a spiker or not—after all these years."

"Honey," said Aunt Winnie, "he never pays a bit of attention to me. It's like I'm not even around half the time. Really. It's God's truth." Her voice broke.

"Aw come on," said Uncle Rory. "That's what half the women in the world say about their husbands, but half the time it's not true. I'm around."

"You may be around, but you're not there," said Aunt Winnie, "if you know what I mean."

"When we were growing up, you were always the one in outer space," Dean's mother said to Rory. "You used to admit it too." She had a smile playing on her lips.

"Hell . . . well, you know. I was a space cadet of sorts, but this is different, see, because Winnie is charging me with something that's just not true. I've seen her spike her drink. I've seen it on more than one occasion. I'm more observant than you give me credit for. You," he said to Aunt Winnie, "and you too," he said to Cousin Gere.

"Wouldn't know," said Gere, "been off fighting wars."

"And darned good thing you have been," said Uncle Rory, patting his shoulder. "Somebody's got to."

"Bravo," said Great Uncle Tommy.

"Damned straight on that one," said Cousin Gere. "Only right now I'm more interested in Beam than in discussing that."

"I'll just take a little of the rum—you buy rum?" Aunt Winnie asked Gere.

"Wasn't me. George bought it—whatever he bought."

"Plenty of rum," shouted out Great Uncle George.

"Well, then, I'll take a little of that rum in my Coke. Okay?" she said to Dean's mother.

"Of course it's okay. You think she's going to say no?" said Uncle Rory.

"No, she's not going to say no, silly," said Aunt Winnie, slapping him, laughing.

"You two," said Cousin Gere.

"He likes his old dad," said Uncle Rory. He put his arm around Cousin Gere. "He likes his old dad, don't you, son?"

"Yeah, I like my old dad," said Cousin Gere, and flushed red.

"Dean, help me with the drinks," said his mother.

"Jean, I'd be happy to help," said Rory.

"No, you stay seated."

Dean was in the kitchen now—along with Great Uncle George, who was lining up glasses and arranging the liquor bottles in a row.

Dean stopped to count—seven pints, two quarts, three bottles of champagne. He noticed the empty paper sacks in the trash.

He was getting out ice when Jennifer and Ginger stepped into the kitchen, saying they'd like to help. Jennifer was a cousin on his mother's side, the daughter of one of her married sisters. She and her friend Ginger were in related fields of study, but his mother didn't know exactly what. Maybe while he and Cousin Gere and Great Uncle George were out getting the booze, they'd gotten into this matter, and he'd missed it.

Dean was afraid he would get too interested in Jennifer, and Ginger as well, eyeing them sexually, and here Jennifer was his first cousin, a luscious looking creature, a grown woman since the last time he'd seen her—how many years ago was that? And Ginger her friend. My, my. So pretty, so . . . fetching. Well, he had a girlfriend. But even so . . .

"We can sure use your help," said Dean's mother. "Right, Dean?"

"That's right."

Dean continued getting the ice out of the ice bag, dumping it into the ice bucket.

"Do we have all the orders?" asked his mother.

"Oh, no, we sure don't," said Jennifer, and placed a hand on Dean's shoulder, causing a buzz in his groin. He fought against it.

"Are you listening, dear?" asked his mother.

"What?"

"Drink orders. Who are we missing?"

Great Uncle George jumped in. "You don't have mine, but then, you don't need it, Jean, since I'll make my own. I'll just uncork one of these champagne bottles here—and see if I can get a little party caucus going out there. Carry a few extra glasses along for good measure . . . where's the corkscrew, Jean?"

She reached in a drawer, pulled it out and held it up.

Great Uncle George took it and smiled.

"Well, there we go. Pop this thing off, and we'll have us a swell time. Thanks, ma'am." He gave Dean a sly wink. "I'm sorry, but I'm the kind of guy who never leaves the important stuff of life to others—always make your own is my motto. Anyway, Jean, I've got a good ear, and I can tell you that you know Rory's, Winnie's, Gere's—"

"Oh, I *know* that," said Dean's mother. "I just got those."

"Well," said Great Uncle George, "what we *don't* know is what Sal wants, or what Tom, or rather Tommy, in there wants, or what Jennifer or Ginger, Jean—you too. What do you want, Jean?"

"Well," said Dean's mother, "I trust we can attend to that ourselves—most of those on your drink list are gathered right here. Except for Uncle Tommy. And Aunt Sally—"

"Sal!" yelled Great Uncle George from the kitchen. "What'll it be in there? What to drink?"

Silence.

"Sal?"

"I don't care. Just anything," she said, with a kind of lugubrious ring to it. Dean turned to look. No smile, sober looking, almost sedate. Yes, sedate. He would use that word. Had she taken one of those pills Great Uncle George spoke of? He noticed the smile lines in her face. They seemed distorted somehow, as though she were about to frown but hadn't quite got there.

"No, honey," shouted Great Uncle George. "Give us something definite in here to work with. *Just anything* is hard to fix. Okay, babe?"

Babe? At that age? Sixty-nine? And Great Uncle George, wasn't he around that age too? Older even?

"I'll take . . . just a minute," and Dean saw her giggling. She was giggling with Aunt Winnie, and the two seemed to be in some sort of cahoots together there on that sofa. "Oh, just make it rum and Coke," she yelled back. Her voice was scratchy, but not sour. In fact, if Dean hadn't known better, he would have thought she might have already imbibed. Good. Because he didn't want a scene. He wasn't a man who liked scenes. It wasn't in him to like them.

"Rum and Coke it is," rang out Great Uncle George. "Think I'll try one myself. Oh, Jean?"

"Yes, George?"

"Leave that corkscrew there. I'll need it presently."

"Oh, of course. Nobody's going to take your corkscrew."

"Ah, good!" said Great Uncle George. "But first, those rum and Cokes."

Dean's mother looked a bit harried. "George, would you mind getting—"

"Why no! Indeed not!" Great Uncle George grabbed two drink glasses and got busy. "And I'll go get Tommy's order here in a minute, and we'll get this show on the road. I'm thinking if Tommy knows anything at all, he knows his booze. I'll go and see what I can find out—and then, you can make his drink, or who knows, maybe he'll want to horn in and fix it himself. Looks to me like a man who makes his own way in this world—doesn't he, Dean?"

"Uh, yes," said Dean. He had the distinct impression that Tom or Tommy did if anyone did.

He watched as Great Uncle George left with two glasses filled nearly to the brim. He handed one to Great Aunt Sally, then stood speaking to Great Uncle Tommy, who was shaking his head. Then he bent over and placed his glass on the floor and returned to the kitchen in a flash. He grabbed up the corkscrew and the champagne bottle. "You have some flutes?" he asked Dean's mother.

"Right above your head," she said, pointing to the cabinet.

He grabbed several champagne flutes, gripping them in one hand.

"No one's opted for champagne—yet," Dean's mother pointed out.

"No, but they will soon, dear," rang out Great Uncle George. "Give them time!" He headed into the living room.

"Two drinks? Well," said Dean's mother. She laughed, and shook her head.

As his mother, Jennifer, and Ginger worked on the drinks, Dean stood by and watched while Great Uncle Tommy strolled into the kitchen. "Just bottled water for me, Jean. I'm not a drinker this early in the day. A cold bottled water would do me about now. Pure spring if you've got it."

"Dean, you want to get that?" asked his mother, working away with the drinks, with Jennifer to one side, Ginger to the other.

"Sure," said Dean.

"My husband sure wouldn't," said Ginger, in a brassy alto. "But I'd make him."

"You direct that poor man about," said Jennifer, in her tingly soprano.

"We've got to make these just right," his mother said. "And the bowls for the snack crackers. They're up there," she said, pointing.

Jennifer went for them.

Dean handed a bottled water to Great Uncle Tommy.

The large man uncapped it, took a long drink, and said, "Well, that does hit the spot. What're you drinking, Dean?"

A beer, of course. He reached into the refrigerator and pulled one out. "Beer," he said. "Beer does it every time."

Damn! He hadn't meant to say that. Why had he said it?

Great Uncle Tommy looked at him and smiled. "I hear you're in school, working on your master's."

"Uh, yes, I am."

"And not far from completion either. When does that degree get earned?" Tommy held his bottled water before him.

"Uh . . . once I get finished with the thesis—at the end of this semester . . . I hope." But he knew that that couldn't possibly be, with only a month or so to spare. He'd just been ignoring that fact, engaging in magical thinking. "If things go well, you know. Always a hitch possible here and there, but you do your best—" Why had he said that—a *hitch*. Damn it! It was Great Uncle Tommy who was making him react so falsely—false to who he normally was. Or really was.

"Sure you do." Great Uncle Tommy took a swig of bottled water. "What's your thesis about, Dean? If you don't mind my asking . . . you're in what area? Was it geography, anthropology—"

"History."

"Ah, history. Yes, that's what Jean said."

His mother turned around from fixing drinks. "He's a very good student, aren't you, Dean? An honor student."

"Well," said Dean. "Yes—a few times."

"A's?" shouted Gere from the living area.

"Yes," said Dean.

"Well now!" said Uncle Rory.

"Rory wasn't exactly a model student in his own time," said Aunt Winnie. "Were you, dear?"

"Those days are long gone," said Rory.

"The past is past," said Great Uncle George, sipping his drink.

"I didn't do so well in history, myself," said Jennifer. "History was just facts, names, dates, places—I felt lucky to remember *anything*, and those tests—multiple choice. All of the Above, Some of the Above, Half of the Above, One Third of the Above. Two thirds! Please!"

"You're good at what you do, though," said Ginger. "She teaches the Art of Social Graces. Just like me."

Dean heard the capitalizations. But was that a real area? In what broader discipline might that be?

"Well, I *do* try," said Jennifer, and looked over at Dean and winked.

There went that buzz in his groin again, but he worked to avoid it. First cousin, that's who she was. He'd never tell Jill about this. And now, he was doubting whether he should invite Jill to this thing—really, should he? On the other hand, if Jill *were* here, maybe it would be different, her sandwiched between him and this Jennifer beauty queen, who was what his mother called a looker. "That cousin of yours," his mother had told him, "when she arrives, she's a real looker, Dean, a heartbreaker. I bet you'll agree. Don't you go kissing her!" What? That was odd. Did his mother intend to break him and Jill up? "Jill's *so* intellectual," his mother often told him. "Do you really want a girl like that?"

"Yes," said Dean. "Why wouldn't I?"

"I wonder what your father would think. Some of the things she says, Dean."

Jill was a hole-poker. An iconoclast. That's what disturbed his mother. She was pretty down on it.

"Well," Jill told her, "I just happen to have a body *and* a mind."

"Are you suggesting," said Dean's mother, "that I don't?"

Jill didn't answer questions like that. At least not from his mother.

Did Jennifer? Was there a mind in that pretty head of hers?

"What's your thesis on?" Great Uncle Tommy was now asking. "That's the bone crusher for many a grad student. Was for me. I didn't think I'd finish that little baby ever, but somehow, you know, you do get the job done. Didn't have to be great, just had to be done. That's the old saying, isn't it?"

Jennifer winked at him. Ginger did too. Damn, but he melted. He looked at Great Uncle Tommy. What was it the man said?

Oh, yes.

"Uh, yeah," said Dean. "That's right. It just has to be done. I've heard that plenty—not like it's going to get published. That takes a lot, more than I've got, honor student or not." He couldn't believe he'd just emphasized being an honor student. He'd been an honor student only a few times, and now, with his total quandary over his thesis, he was certainly *not* an honor student.

"You can do it," rang out Jennifer. "Just put on a big smile and go for it!"

"My husband would drink his way right through it," said Ginger. "And he'd get the job done. You bet!"

Great Uncle Tommy hugged his bottled water. "What's the topic, Dean? That's the key. A great topic. Saves you a lot of grief in the long run. And now with that deadline approaching—"

"Hmm, yeah," said Dean, and he looked at his mother. She had her back to him, arranging drinks on a tray, while Jennifer had some napkins going, and Ginger was going after some decorative toothpicks—red, green, and gold. And his mother was now saying, "Time for the cheese. It's cut up, Ginger. Could you get that? And Jennifer, the crackers are up there, just above your head in that cabinet. And those little plates for each person. And trays to carry things. Oh, and olives in the fridge!" Her voice, Dean thought, sounded seriously strained, and he was now on stage.

Great Uncle Tommy continued to stare at him, obviously expecting an answer. He was smiling, just slightly, as though he weren't one to push a man. He had skills in the Social Graces, Dean could see that. And he wished he had more himself, but oftentimes all he could do was croak out what was on his heart and mind. And now, pressed for an answer, he was about to say something that might disturb things, making him a boat-rocker, a killjoy.

He tried to get it out. "I'm doing . . . well, it's about war, I guess you'd say—"

"Ah, war! Good! Fantastic! That's a great topic, Dean, and my god, with history being what it is, who'd want to pick some topic that made so little difference, given the part that war has always played in the history of mankind. Pick the big ones. Why settle for the little fish. Throw them back! Right?"

"Yes, that's right," said Dean.

And he saw his mother turn around, just slightly, and smile. Was there a tinge of anxiousness in that smile? Were her thin lips trembling? He was one to note trembling lips. His eyes seemed to start there.

Dean spotted Great Uncle George working at the champagne bottle with the corkscrew. He worked and worked at it, and Dean couldn't help but gawk as the heavyset man grunted. Suddenly there was a loud pop, a geyser of red liquid, and Dean witnessed an abrupt movement close by, then a sudden blue whirling, and Cousin Gere emerging out of the whirlwind with his wide hand rocketing out of his pocket.

That shiny black .45.

Cousin Gere now positioning himself in a shooting stance. It somehow recalled to Dean a pointer signaling his prey. It seemed that time itself was bracketed, and then a panic of hysterical shrieks, pleadings, women's wailing voices, and then a deadening silence. Fearful in its utter quietness. And its length.

Gere, Marine, crouching, aiming.

And finally Cousin Gere's spotting the champagne bottle twirling in the air above Great Uncle George's head, clutched by the aged

40

hand, but still that .45 aimed, Cousin Gere now with a studied look, something like apprehension mixed with die-hard deliberateness, and then Great Uncle George, in a kind of soothing voice: "Hey, Gere, hey, bud ... it's just a champagne bottle ... see? Hell, man, the fruit of the vine. Not the best brand they had, but hell fire—" A nervous giggle from Great Uncle George, then the gradual lowering of the champagne bottle, and a sort of beckoning toward Cousin Gere, Great Uncle George smiling brightly, but still that gun.

A snarl from Gere.

"Hey, no need to—no need, see—"

"What the fuck?" shouted Cousin Gere. "What're you trying to pull, chief?"

"Oh, no, I didn't mean—"

"What the fuck you trying to pull?" Cousin Gere's hand shook.

"No, see, it just happened. Too close, yeah, but—"

"Yeah, too close," sneered Gere. And there was still that gun, steady on Great Uncle George. Would it go off? When? Where? The gut, it looked like.

"Son," said Uncle Rory. "Son, please—"

"Honey, *please*," whined Aunt Winnie.

"May I intercede?" asked Jennifer.

"And I?" asked Ginger.

"Yeah, what?" said Cousin Gere.

"To implore you," said Jennifer, taking him by the arm.

"To implore you not to fire your weapon in a crowd," said Ginger. "To holster it."

"Safety," said Jennifer. "Safety is paramount."

"I don't know *why*," sighed Cousin Gere. "Don't know why. Damn well *don't* know why!"

"There is much we don't know," said Jennifer.

"Much we'll never know," said Ginger.

Great Uncle Tommy now into the fray. "Weapon safety—yes, sir, Gere, the women are spot on. That is one thing we do know. Take it from a Weapons Man."

Dean heard the capitalizations. Clearly. They were there.

Then the .45 slowly being lowered, a blank look on Gere's face, and then the .45 being pocketed. And finally a grin of sorts coming over his lips—was it malicious?—then a little abrasive snicker to match it, and: "Well, hell . . . thought we were under attack there, folks. Dammit, George, you gotta give a man a little warning there— mother fuck!!!"

"Whew!" said Great Uncle George. "I meant a party by this. Didn't mean a—"

"Ambush?" said Cousin Gere. But then he got a perturbed look on his face. He sat down. "I'll take a little of that to go with the other," he said.

"Sure do think you need it," said Great Uncle George. "Smooth off the edges a bit."

"A good idea!" shouted Uncle Rory.

"Oh, god," said Aunt Winnie. "Oh, dear god!"

Sally. Dear god, that Sally. Trembling blue lips. A trembling hand. Her eyes zoned out.

Great Uncle Tommy returned to the kitchen. He shook his head at Dean, smiled, then took a swig of his bottled water. He rubbed his long, clean-shaven chin as though deliberating. "Well, well. My, my. Umm. Now . . . where were we, Dean?" Then he said: "Oh, yes. Yes. And so what are you planning on doing with your topic? My god, about everything in the world has been written on war, books and books and books on the first one, the second, the Civil War—what's left to say? I'm sure there's something, or the historians would have to lock their offices up and go home and retire and study their belly buttons, but what *is* left to say? You're the historian. What would that be?"

"Umm," said Dean.

Great Uncle Tommy smiled. "Well, here it is April, and the semester end draweth nigh, sir, so surely—"

"I've got stuff—lots of it," said Dean, downing beer. And downing more. He felt it flow down into his being, and wished he were in that beer, flowing to some hidden place. He felt under attack.

"Stuff?" said Tommy. "What sort of stuff, Mr. Dean?"

Dean paused. He felt compelled of a sudden. Energized even. "Notebooks—notebooks being filled. Or, well, one notebook, that is. Yes, one. More than half-filled. I'm telling you, I . . . yeah, man, I mean—"

"Notebooks," said Great Uncle Tommy. "No chapters yet?"

"No."

Great Uncle Tommy smiled a fatherly smile. "Dean, sir, you've got to decide and hurry the process along. Get that degree. Get it while you can. I put mine off, was fully employed, trying to hack out a living, day to day, every day, and it was really hard to hit those books, do that thesis—so do it now while you've got the time. Before you take on the added responsibility of job, wife, and family. Believe me, partner, that'll go a long way, as you'll see, down the road. Won't it, Jean?"

"Oh, yes!" said his mother. And Dean watched her pivoting around with a tray balanced in her arms, full of snacks and drinks, and nodding. "A long way. Finish the degree. Do it now," she said, her voice jumpy and jittery. "Yes."

"Good!" said Uncle Tommy. "So. War. *Which* war we talking about, Dean? *And* the point you'd be making. Or the point the scholars would be making. I guess it comes down to that. But first, where are *you* in this thing, Dean? That was the question my old prof asked me when I did my thesis on technology. 'Where are you, Mr. Gumm, on this new burst of technology? This whole new paradigm shift?' Well, I had to put on my thinking cap, and believe me, Dean, believe me, it helped to know where *I* was, how it affected *my* life, before I could understand exactly what all the scholars out there writing articles and books really meant. Where they were going with it all. See? Don't you think?"

Dean nodded. "I do think. I think you're right about that."

"So . . ." asked Great Uncle Tommy, placing a hand on Dean's shoulder, "where's the starting point for Dean Troost. And maybe . . . the ending point? Those were the two questions, and very good ones, my own thesis prof asked me. So, to help you along, I'll ask those of you." He smiled slyly—it was a mischievous looking smile, a father-son smile. Or grandfather-grandson—yes, more like that.

Dean drank more beer. A couple gulps. A few more. What to say? He said nothing.

"Oh, come on now," said Great Uncle Tommy, "we're all friends here—blood relatives in one way or another!—so don't worry how you answer. Just do a little brainstorming. Right out loud. Give it a go, son. I'm here to help. To get that degree!"

Dean felt fueled.

"Well, I *started*," he began, clearing his throat, "with all the war dead. So many over the centuries. So many. Too many. Each and every one of them dead. Dead, dead, *dead*. Bloody, mangled, guts hanging out, legs blown off, arms blown off, feet, heads blown off, balls blown off—Jeez Louise!"

"Great!" cried Great Uncle Tommy. "You're at least aware of the cost. A true trooper, you are. I wonder how many are. But, then, where—where did you go with that? Or are going? Or plan to go?"

Dean's tongue went dead.

Great Uncle Tommy had him fixed, wriggling.

He looked about. They were all looking his way. They had apparently stopped their own conversations and were now waiting to hear him. He felt public. Gere sneering. Jennifer and Ginger smiling. Great Uncle George, Uncle Rory, and Aunt Winnie attentive. Great Aunt Sally despairing.

His mother? He noticed her unloading a tray of snacks and drinks in the living room. For a second she turned to look at him. Square on. There was harsh invective in that look—he could imagine acid dripping off her tongue. If she spoke, it'd be a snap and a snarl.

"Well, sir?" asked Tommy.

He must respond. He must proceed.

"I . . . haven't," said Dean. "I'm stuck . . . with that. With the millions—the hundreds of millions over millennia—it must be hundreds of millions. More!"

"That may be true," said Great Uncle Tommy. "I never thought of it that way."

And now, in spite of his mother, Dean did proceed.

"Yes—*and* now here's this big war." Okay . . . okay he'd said it, but he didn't care now because *he* hadn't started this business; it was Great Uncle Tommy pushing, pushing. And he didn't want to be misunderstood, to leave anything important out. He wanted clarity, brilliant clarity, no hedging, no fudging, no mealy-mouthing. Dead, dead, dead. All of them. In the ground. Unconscious. No brain, no mind. "Honey," Jill said, "I know I'm one of the few, but I do think the mind is more than the brain."

"But Jill," he said. "How? What if it's not?"

"It is," she said, with a confidence that seemed rather gullible to him.

"So many dead," he went on. "Over a million already, with the numbers climbing. And, see, here's the thing—here's the f-ing—"

"Dean, Dean," said Great Uncle Tommy. "What you say is true. Of course it's true. But the biggest percent of those are on the other side. Not ours."

Dean felt his insides now quaking, and finished off his beer in one long swallow and turned toward the refrigerator and went for another. He lifted the tab, took a huge gulp, and he saw Tommy staring at him. "War's outmoded," he said. "We've had enough of it. Haven't we now?" He liked the way this came out. It sounded authoritative. There was a commanding air about it that made him feel cocky, of a sudden.

In came Gere. "Couldn't help but hear what the two of you were talking about. Tommy. Dean. If you think that war is outmoded or something, you're flat out wrong, chief." He came up closer to Dean, and poked a finger at his chest. A second poke. A third. Hard, painful pokes, each of them. "I'd like to see you get away from it. You got the blood lust in most peckers' eyes. You got the blood lust in your own, I'll betcha. Tell me what Sunday School picnic's going to solve that one? Huh?"

Another poke, even harder.

Tommy leaned back, seeming to appreciate this. "Oh, well," he laughed, "we may be heading toward an impasse here. But just so you know, Dean, I'd have to vote with Gere on that one. You're not going to do away with war anytime soon. Only consider what the Good Book says. Wars and rumors of wars. Not something they talk about a lot in Sunday School, as Gere mentioned, and don't think they should either, but it's there—it's not going to change just because we want it to. And maybe it shouldn't. It blows off a lot of steam, in my opinion. Probably people'd eat themselves alive without it. The keg blows, and you get things back to normal. In that way, war's a good thing."

"Affirm," said Cousin Gere. "When you blow the Bad Mother Fuckers to Kingdom Come."

Indisputable capitalizations, thought Dean. "But a million of them dead," he screeched, his hackles raised, "in this big bad war we've got going—and well, hell . . ." Phlegm now in his voice— it definitely wasn't there before. He could hardly talk, his voice cracking, croaking. It suddenly flashed at him: be brusque! "What the fuck's going on!" he yelled. "What the f-ing fuck!"

Tommy flinched, stood back, his eyes wide. And then rubbed a finger on his upper lip.

Gear grinned, snarled.

Great Uncle Tommy laid a hand on Dean's wrist. "Hmm? Well, Dean, it *is* food for thought. Who can dispute it? But like I just mentioned, a very small proportion of that number represents our own brave men and women in uniform. Isn't that right, Gere? Maybe we've hit the one thousandth of a percent mark, you reckon?"

"Damned straight," said Gere, sipping his drink. "The losses are on the Other Side, and in my book, that's the Wrong Side. *Wrong Side*, ace. When they're on the Right Side, on God's side if you're the religious type, well, hell, then I'll listen. But as long as they're on the Wrong Side, leave me out of it. I don't care. I fucking, flat out don't care."

Dean could see Aunt Winnie wanting to intervene. She was waving a hand.

"Yes, ma'am," said Great Uncle Tommy.

"One thing I can tell you for sure," said Aunt Winnie. "Our son's on the Right Side. Right, dear?" She turned to Uncle Rory.

"If there's a Right Side, he's on it," said Rory.

"Of course, there's a Right Side!" said Aunt Winnie, slapping his hand, with a grin.

"Tell you what," said Great Uncle George, "that's the only side to be on. You can tell by the medals. There's your dead ringer."

Jennifer popped up. "A man with medals has much to smile about. Pride is good if it's well deserved."

"Even if it isn't, there's nothing wrong with pride," said Ginger.

"Well, that's right," said Jennifer. "Have pride. Start there."

Great Aunt Sally was viewing the ceiling. What was up there? Dean looked but saw only the popcorn white surface.

"All good ideas," said Great Uncle Tommy. "All to the good." And then he laid a hand on Gere's wrist. "Lookit," he said, "such matters as these, especially when it's war, are always heated, and should be. We come to the table with our own stake in them—you, Gere, a soldier, you, Dean, a student—me a weapons manufacturer. I could say 'We'll agree to disagree,' and I'd be right. Right? But the main thing is that we shake hands on it and have a drink and put the matter aside. Gere?"

Gere nodded. He extended his hand for a shake. It was a hard shake, too hard, and Dean pulled his hand loose. That grip could crush bones. Gere must have used one of those gripping devices Dean had seen advertised on the Internet. Or maybe it was the Marines. Yes, of course, it was the Marines. Hard men, hard.

Great Uncle Tommy shook both their hands, a firm but gentle shake. "I'd like to end this discussion with one little addendum," he said, looking first at Cousin Gere, then at Dean. "Of course running a division at a weapons plant, you'd think I have a real stake in things. And I do. But I don't think *only* like a weapons manufacturer. I'm a husband, father, uncle, *great* uncle—all the rest, filling many roles, you see, just as any man does, and I have my hobbies, my gardening, for instance, my love of golfing, my boating, fishing, hunting, deep sea diving—not swimming with sharks yet, but anyway, the list is endless. I'm a man of many interests, I guess you'd say. And I love people. I'm a real people person. I love a reunion like this. I'm a regular joiner just because I love people. I'm in any number of service organizations, church activities, social clubs—I'm so busy I can't find a minute even to brush my teeth, only I do it. Don't worry about that!" He gave them a laugh, then a sly grin. "But beyond all this, I do believe that war, this present war included, is quite necessary. Sure, there's been suffering of untold proportions on both sides, the smashing of various cities, the killing of civilians, women, children, collateral damage or what have you, but we've got to see it for what it is: renewal. Redemption of a kind. And unless we are into redemption, we'll never understand much of what life is all about. We'll never understand God Himself. Isn't that right, Gere?"

A silence. And Dean watched Cousin Gere's face turn orange-red.

He stomped a boot on the kitchen floor. "I get fucking *tired*," he shouted, "of the fucking morons who don't understand what it is to *be* fucking there. Oh, you can sit at home and ease back in your fucking recliner and watch your fucking TV with your fucking beer in your fucking hand and criticize, but you *be* fucking there. You just fucking *be* there, and you just fucking see what you think then!" He took off, pivoting on one boot, hurry marching, his medals jingling. Then he pivoted again and faced them. Dean thought he caught a glint of orange sunlight flickering off those medals.

Dean was impressed by how dexterously Cousin Gere could pivot, actually turning on one boot. He thought Gere would be a fierce opponent in a tackle football game, taking on any of the athletic frat jocks out there he'd seen.

"Damn, son!" shouted Uncle Rory, as Gere reclaimed his seat.

"Oh, dear, dear," moaned Aunt Winnie.

"Whew!" said Great Uncle Tommy. "He's a piece of dynamite, *n'est-ce pas?*"

3

Jennifer, seated on one of the folding chairs, smiled at Dean as he approached her. He saw no other place to sit but beside her on a folding chair next to the door. He moseyed over, with a plate of crackers, cheese, olives, and his beer in his right hand. He felt somewhat exposed. But at least, he thought, he had something in his hands, something to keep him from facing Jennifer, this delectable dish, all alone, with no resources.

"Sit down," she beckoned.

Dean did as directed. Smiled. Pretty girls made him quite nervous. He would almost prefer that they not be pretty. Except with Jill, but they were past all that. And so it was different.

"So . . . you're working on your thesis. Such a challenge!"

"Yes," he said. "It is."

He could see his mother on the other side of the room, jabbering away at Great Aunt Sally, Aunt Winnie, Uncle Rory, and Cousin Gere. In his own little party caucus was Ginger, who was speaking fast and furiously at Great Uncle George, who was nodding and *Ah-ha-ing*, stopping to pour more champagne into his flute. Great Uncle Tommy was sitting back, his hands poised in his lap, with a smile creeping over his lips. Now and then he'd take a sip of his bottled water.

"Well, better you than me," said Jennifer, with a girlish giggle. "Like I said in there"—she pointed at the kitchen—"I'm not so good at history. Pardon me for saying so, but I just find it boring." She tucked a wet olive between her moist red lips. "All those times past, and all those people dead and gone. You see what I mean, don't you? It's old, tired. We've been through it. Let's move on now, for god's sake! Is that just being totally silly, or what?"

How to answer that? "Well," said Dean. "I suppose I can see that." He couldn't, though. But he wanted to be nice, cool, not critical. He wished he could light up a cigarette or maybe a cigar, or even a pipe, and offer an off-the-cuff remark, and then let a volley of gray smoke out. He'd wave the air and laugh, and she would too.

But he wasn't a smoker, and his mother wouldn't permit it in the apartment. He inserted a wheat cracker, snapped it between two front teeth, and began to crunch. And then he took a quick swig of beer. He made a tentative wipe at his lips, leery of crumbs.

"Oh, surely that's not how you feel. You're so steeped in it. I'll just bet."

True. He'd always loved history. But here she was bored with it. How could he infuse in her the same feeling he got when he entered its pages, lived right along with all those who were swept along by the tide of economic, political, social, and military events, crushed so often, but now and then triumphant, only to be subject in a generation or so to more of the same, some sort of unrelenting push toward what? He didn't know. Toward doom? Sometimes he felt that way. Doom? And yet from the time he'd taken his first history course at university, he had thought that *this* is what he wanted to know. He wanted to fill in where the blank spots occurred. Somehow, if he could just piece it all together, he'd have a handle on understanding what it was all about. And maybe, though his thesis director, Harry, told him he was being overdramatic to think so, he'd learn what he himself was about. Well, it sounded good. Jill told him it did. "Go for it, darling," she said. Whenever she called him darling, he got a big buzz in his groin. He couldn't help it. But Harry: "That's not history, Dean," he chided. "That's the humanities—so, sir, I'd suggest switching your major."

"Um," said Dean. How could he? Start over?

"I didn't mean to offend," Jennifer said.

"No, no," he said. "No. I'm not offended. I'm just the history buff kind of guy." Oh, hell! He hated that word *buff*. Why did he have to say that—because she was so pretty, and he was so rattled?

"Well, and that's good that there *are* people like you," Jennifer said. "Because what would it be like if there were absolutely no historians? I mean, I ask that about myself and what I do. Not everyone would want to do it, but it's good that I do it, I guess, or at least I think it is. I don't know. Sometimes, really, I'm just not sure—"

"What do you do?" And then he remembered: "Oh, the Art of Social—"

"Graces. Yes—but that's oversimplifying it. It really is—actually it's totally a misnomer. It's not just the *art*—you see—since it's a university discipline; I'm into the theory as well, of course. As is Ginger. But on the practical side, we're both personal trainers, of sorts. I *guess* you could say that. And this includes the whole physical person, and the way he or she comports himself or herself. We're very comprehensive—even physical fitness fits in there."

"Umm. Physical fitness," Dean said. He felt flabby all of a sudden. His gut pushed out a little, and he wanted to push it back in—but in front of Jennifer? He wished, like the athletic frat jocks that he often saw on the campus grounds, that he could get more physically fit, and he often told himself he'd get up and run, lift weights, and— the next time he played ball with Harry and the grad students— he'd catch a pass for damned once. "You're no athletic frat jock," said Jill. "Besides I hate them. Vacuous. Bestial."

"Um," he said. "Yeah." It made him feel better.

"Yes—of sorts," Jennifer was saying. And she inserted another wet olive between bright white teeth, then eased down on it with those luscious red lips of hers. It was a green olive, stuffed with pimiento. Cheap—he'd bought them cheap, trying, as his mother had urged, to save money. The EatRite brand. "I train in any number of physical aspects of the whole person—including correct *posture* in the very largest sense: which includes among other things, how to enter a room, how to sit—notice how I'm sitting right now, for instance . . . erect, back straight, neck just so . . . I also teach how to lie down in bed to get a good night's sleep, how to comport—I actually *do* use that word, Dean—oneself when standing and having a conversation . . . there are both informal and formal poses. But all for good health, good well-being, good manners too, general points of politeness and *respect*, because you know, Dean, how it is to be around someone who invades your personal space, especially if this person leans in toward you, gets right up to you . . . speaks *at* you. *In your face.* But . . . how pleasing it is if this person is in command of

51

his or her posture—in the largest sense of that word—in command of the space, taking only his or her own, not yours too, and fills that space with . . . and I do use this word, Dean—*decorum*. Sort of lost to our contemporary world, but there it is. I use it, and some others are getting into the practice of using it too. I guess because after the general trashiness of the world following the various sexual and social revolutions and the end of the century dumping on us the tattooed, the impaled, the personally mutilated—I'm talking huge holes in ears the size of quarters you can see right through, pieces of metal stuck in tongues, ears, and belly buttons—well, we're feeling a need for some kind of personal hygiene. Some sort of personal decency. A well-executed delivery of the Social Graces!" She drew a breath, a quick desperate one, and took a sip of her hard drink. She smiled. "Sorry for the long-winded oration! It's kind of my spiel. I guess I've practiced it enough at meetings, personal training sessions for K-12 schools, colleges, universities, corporate team-building, etcetera, etcetera. Anyway, the short of it is, we want to be better people. Or at least *behave* like we're better people—how's that?"

Dean tried to take it all in. He crunched a wheat snack cracker, nodded just to be polite, and he was reminded of Great Uncle George nodding at Ginger, although he himself wasn't saying *Ah-ha!*

"Well," said Jennifer, "after all that, give me some feedback, Dean. Oh, do. Gosh, I just bared my whole soul to you!"

Damn but that buzz in his groin again! Maybe it was that word *bared* that did it, and especially the look in Jennifer's lovely blue eyes. She was a real beauty queen all right. He could imagine her helping others achieve a perfect posture in that largest sense, and how to be appropriate in the way they spoke to others. But he was having trouble carrying this further, thinking of anything intelligent to add. "So you like it," he said. "Doing this." He fumbled for another word or two, but nothing came out.

She seemed to consider this. "Yes—I think so. I do it several hours a day. Especially for the young ladies. And maybe your mother told you: Ginger and I will be on stage tonight at a fundraiser for the troops—but I won't say any more about that because, well, I happen to know about a little surprise in that regard, so . . . mum's the word." She blushed. "Anyway, I tell you, Dean, this is coming back. Big time. There's a whole movement afoot, as though we were living in another age, when people—people who have a little money—want to get their kids out of the mall for a moment, get them away from the video games, the TV, and get them into social intercourse—I call it that. People grin when I use that word, thinking of the other." She laid a hand on Dean's arm, and smiled, and there again that buzz in his groin, but much worse this time, and she said, "but really, I can see *why*. They realize that to make it in today's world, you've got to be a cut above everyone else. A little charm, politeness, grace—these go a long way in an interview for a high-powered job, the six-figure kind. Take two people with the same creds—who will the employer of the hotsy-totsy corp hire? The one who puts on a good show. Naturally. Knows how to *smile* . . . for instance." She lingered on that one word for a moment, as though relishing it with the next olive she now inserted between her moist red lips and perfectly straight, white teeth.

"Aha!" said Dean.

"There's *a lot* in a smile," said Jennifer, and she took a sip of her hard drink. "I'll bet I spend two weeks on the art of smiling alone—sometimes more." She waited, apparently for some reaction from Dean.

He had none. Other than, "Well—"

"Yes—two weeks," she said. "Sometimes more. The *sometimes more* is for those who don't have the slightest clue of how to smile. They don't seem aware of the smile lines in their face, just where these are, what they do—what tremendous effects they can have. They think there's just a smile, you crack it, and that's it. Wrong. That's just plain wrong."

"Umm," said Dean.

Jennifer now smiled at him, heavy and long, apparently, he thought, trying out the perfect smile. There was something in it, and he'd have to puzzle it out. What *was* behind it? "You can tell what's behind a smile if there *is* anything behind it," Jill told him. "Look close. Is there anything there, or just a face? Is there a *mind*? Ask yourself that. *Is* there one?" Jill was often very critical.

He looked close. For a vagrant second, he wondered. And then he quaked. He was seeing her skin up too close, and it suddenly looked too porous. He imagined deep pits. He tried not to look. "Men," said Jill, "are more inclined than women to take in the body only."

He couldn't help but agree. "But there is the ladder of love," he protested. "Isn't there?"

She laughed. "How many men make it past the first rung?" Jill, his girlfriend, his lover, had a low opinion of men—"But not you," she told him, "I don't mean you." Thank god, he thought.

Jennifer put her fingers up to her lips, as though about to obliterate that smile. "You don't smile a lot," she told Dean. "And I've been watching you ever since you sat down. It's a habit of mine. I can't help it. Just like you probably can't help grabbing a history book in the bookstore, and pointing out slavery or war, or torture, well . . . I can't help watching for signs and symptoms of the smile function in people. I've trained myself. Did you know I started by working for a dermatologist?"

"No."

"That's right. That's where it all started. But I wasn't happy with that. I wanted—"

Ginger was flashing a large, glossy photo at them. Great Uncle George was nodding fiercely.

"Oh!" shouted Jennifer.

Dean saw it. Ginger and a large beefy man, pictured in the glossy eight-by-ten, were kneeling with a deer with an eight-point rack, their arms around the dead animal like they were all about to say cheese.

"You and that husband of yours!" shouted Jennifer. "Now there's a smile for you, Dean! Just observe!"

"Yes, dear, I do smile when recollecting this particular event," said Ginger, and for a moment Dean thought the woman was about to cry. But she didn't, and she came forth with another photo, even larger, a ten-by-twelve, maybe, also glossy, catching the sun through the blinds with a flash of light. It was a huge bear, downed, with Ginger and her husband each resting a boot on its furry body. "It took us three days up in Alaska to bring down this big sweetheart, but we got him—you bet."

"Big game," said Jennifer. "She loves the big hunt, don't you, Ginger?"

"They don't call it game for nothing," said Ginger. "Strategy!"

"And she's a big meat eater too," said Jennifer.

"You as well," said Ginger.

"Oh, I admit it."

"Bear?" said Dean.

"If cooked well, it's great!" said Ginger.

"I'm a vegetarian myself," said Dean.

Ginger's eyes narrowed in on him. "My husband would say, 'Oh, are you? Know ye not about domination?' I have words for those crypto-fascist animal lovers, Dean, sir!" She giggled, and spun around when Great Uncle George laid a hand on her wrist.

"The Good Book," spoke up Great Uncle George. "It's all in there. We mustn't question it. Hey!"

"Blood sacrifice," said Ginger. "We all got a love for it, you bet. The thrill of the kill!"

"Now, now," said Great Uncle George. "But . . . well, I am taken back to my old hunting days. The pistol, the rifle, the bow!"

There was a loud "Fuck!" in the room. And then "Goddamn it! I mean it, goddamn it! Fuck!"

"What's that?" said Jennifer and strained to look.

Dean looked.

Great Uncle George and Ginger looked. Great Uncle Tommy looked.

It was Cousin Gere, who was now poised like an attack dog at Dean's mother.

"Son!" said Uncle Rory.

"Honey, please!" cried Aunt Winnie.

55

"No, you fucking listen here," shouted Cousin Gere. He poked her arm with his finger. Poke, poke. Poke, poke. "You listen *here*. I showed up at this old lady's afternoon tea, but I don't fucking have to stay. And hear that shit. I showed up, but there's a limit to what I'll hear. You follow me?" His face was now against hers. Cheek to cheek, jowl to jowl. Was he going to bite her? Gut punch her? Hurl her across the room like a rag doll?

Gun.

It was out.

Pointed up.

A sharp bark, like a door slamming.

A second one.

A third.

Hole!

Hole in the ceiling!

"Got your attention, folks? Fucking A!"

"Gere!" That was Uncle Rory.

"Son!" That was Aunt Winnie.

"What the—?" shouted Dean. He moved into the fray.

Cousin Gere stepped aside from Dean's mother, pocketing that .45.

"Fucking A. Got that ceiling's attention!"

"You can put your hand right through that!" shouted Rory. "Look!"

"Son!" shouted Winnie.

"Gere," said Great Uncle Tommy. "Listen here. Control, sir. Control."

Jennifer and Ginger had arrived. They were both, Dean observed, wagging fingers, school teacher fashion. "This lacks the proper decorum," said Jennifer. "I must tell you how I abhor this particular behavior."

"And I," said Ginger. "Barbaric. Isn't it, Jen?"

"Utterly."

"Yeah. Well, you two go sit and stow your bullshit. Got it?"

"We will not," said Ginger.

"Well," said Jennifer, taking her by the arm.

"All right. But this is despicable behavior," said Ginger. They moved off. Dean watched them go back to their chairs.

"What the—?" said Dean, confronting Gere.

"*Her*," said Cousin Gere, "your big-eyed Mommy there . . ."

"What the—?" cried Dean. He stood here before a man who had been on multiple tours of duty in the war, and he was facing him down. "What . . . what did my mother say?"

"Oh!" yelled out his mother, crying. "I said *nothing*. I said nothing at all! Oh, and my ceiling! Look! Just look!"

"Said *nothing*. Yeah? Well . . . I don't goddamned carry this rod for nothing," sneered Cousin Gere, patting his pocket.

"Don't mock," said Aunt Winnie. "You should never mock your aunt. And show some respect. You're in her house, for heaven's sake."

"Thank you, Winnie," said Dean's mother, sobbing.

"Oh, but that ceiling!" cried Winnie.

"Son," said Uncle Rory, rising from the couch. "We have to talk about this, and I think the time is about right now, so if you don't mind—not in here, though, but—"

"Yeah, yeah," said Cousin Gere. "Sure, you bet. We'll talk. We'll fucking A talk. Let's rehearse it. What did you just say, Aunt Jean? Tell them all, all these people assembled here before us, what you just said."

"I said *nothing*," said Dean's mother. "I meant nothing at all by it." She cried harder.

Dean moved an inch closer to Cousin Gere. And he said, in what he thought proudly was a severe voice, no flinching. "What *did* you say? Tell us."

Cousin Gere gave him a shove, not too much of a shove, but enough of one that it counted *as* a shove. There was no question, this *was* a shove. Gere had his face in his face. "You taking charge here, chief? You think you're the one taking charge here, ace?"

"No," said Dean, but he thought, yes, yes, I am because I'm the head of the house. He had too often, he thought, flinched in his life, especially when a bunch of athletic frat jocks scoffed at him for missing a pass on the field when he'd played with the team which included Harry and the other grad students. He hadn't flinched when it was one of the grad students who criticized him, only when one of the athletic frat jocks in their gray frat tee shirts had made certain innuendos regarding his manhood.

"Son," said Uncle Rory, standing by, "let's adjourn into the kitchen and discuss this. Jean's gone to a lot of bother, Dean's gone to a lot of bother—"

"Fucking broke their necks, didn't they?" said Cousin Gere. "Hate to think we put them out big time—well, me, I'm a-hoofing it."

"Wait, wait, please," said Dean's mother, wiping tears streaking down her cheeks. "Please don't go away mad. Honey, please, I've known you since you were just a little tyke, only that high"—and she lowered her hand to six inches or so off the floor.

"Smaller than that," said Aunt Winnie. "Since his babyhood. Remember, you saw him right after—"

"Cut the crap, willya! Goddamn!" growled Cousin Gere, though this comment seemed to have relaxed him somehow. A smile crept across his face, a grimace mixed with a smile, or was it a smirk?

"Let me, Gere—will you just let me? I know you're a big grown man now, in the Army and all—"

"Army! I'm not in the goddamned Army! You fucking listen here—"

"Marines. I meant Marines!"

"Yeah."

"But could I?" and Dean's mother moved in for an embrace and she held him a good long time.

Then Cousin Gere backed off and sat back down.

"All back to normal—good!" said Uncle Rory.

"Well, of course!" said Aunt Winnie. "Oh . . . but, my god, that horrible, that horrible—" She pointed up.

Dean's mother looked up.

Dean looked up.

He looked around. Everyone was looking up.

"Good thing we're on the top floor!" said Dean's mother, laughing. It wasn't much of a laugh, but it was a laugh.

They all laughed.

Dean didn't. He was wondering what was so funny.

Cousin Gere didn't, and Dean stood, fixed in his place, watching him, wondering. What? What? But he knew better than to ask.

After a few moments of standing there, he saw Cousin Gere look up, and then at him.

"You wanting something, ace? Is that why you're parked there like a statue? Well, I'll tell you what she said—your big ole Mommy there. Maybe that's why you're standing there with your dick hanging out. Huh?"

"Gere!" shouted Aunt Winnie. "That's no way—"

"Son," said Uncle Rory. "You really shouldn't—"

Cousin Gere waved them off, like insects buzzing around him. "You ask her, but I doubt she'll tell you. Don't know why, but women like to bury things. Take my Mom—"

"I do not!" said Aunt Winnie.

"Yeah, you do. You damn bet you do," said Cousin Gere.

"Honey," said Uncle Rory. "Let it alone. Okay?"

"So . . . I'll tell you," said Cousin Gere. "I'll just fill your little ears there, Dean-o Boy. Your Mommy there, my *Aunt Jean*, she got to picking over my uniform, you know. You know how women are. They go for bright objects, like these medals here"—he ran his hand over his four rows, which Dean couldn't help but lean forward to study, trying to get a fix on them—"kind of like a squirrel goes for bright objects. Or a crow—"

"Gere!" shouted Aunt Winnie. "That is a terrible, disgraceful thing to say about women—and about your aunt."

"Damn fucking true," said Cousin Gere, with a sly smile on his face. "Who's the ones watching those jewelry shows on TV—is that men, or is it women?"

"You ought to be ashamed, son," said Uncle Rory, but Dean thought he detected a mischievous grin working on the man's lips.

"Never mind that, though," said Cousin Gere. "If it's true, or if it ain't—who the hell cares?" He looked at Dean, and then at Dean's mother, who was standing now with her arms folded across her stomach, righteously indignant. Dean had seen it plenty. His mother was usually one to smooth things over, but she had her cracking point. And that squirrel and/or crow comparison had caused her to reach it. She did not like belittling. In fact, it was one thing he had been raised not to do. "Don't belittle people, honey," she had always told him. "Always find good in people. It's there if you look."

"Look," said Uncle Rory, "I think we ought to put all this aside, start with a clean slate, and move on. Okay, son?"

"I think our son owes his aunt a real apology before there's any moving on," said Aunt Winnie.

There was a buzz of voices in the room, and Dean looked around. Great Uncle George, with Ginger, were all eyes, whispering something at each other as they gawked at what was unfolding before them. Dean felt something coming. The air was heavy with it.

Cousin Gere now stood up, let out a bark of a yell, and the buzz of voices quieted down.

"You hear this, and you hear it well," roared Cousin Gere. "*All* of you. I don't put up with anyone, Aunt This, Aunt That, Cousin This, Cousin That, Uncle whoever the hell you are, calling into question what's behind these medals lined up here on my chest." He beat it with his fist. "You hear?"

"Oh, Gere, I didn't mean—"

"You didn't *mean*. No, you didn't *mean*. Didn't you say, 'Gere,' as you ran your fat fingers over the medals, 'honey . . . that's *a lot*. Look at all of them! But no *Purple Heart*? You didn't get the Purple Fucking Heart?'"

"Now, son, she didn't say that!" said Uncle Rory. "She sure didn't say the f-word with the Purple Heart—I'm quite sure. I know Jean. She didn't say *that*."

"Might as well have," said Cousin Gere. "You think there's not enough goddamn medals here? I got to have the goddamn Purple

60

Heart like your hubby parked over there—that it?" He pointed at the picture of Dean's father, with the Purple Heart draping his chest. "And all I've done for you, for you, for you, for *you*"—Gere twirled around the room, pointing at each and every one of the people assembled. "Fucking Purple Heart, huh? What I did—that didn't *count*? Just 'cause I was smart enough to stay out of the path of the fucking bullets, grenades, mortars, car bombs? Huh? No—they don't award being smart like that! And don't you call it *lucky* either. It was smart! Fast on my feet—tricky moves! *Up here* smart!" Cousin Gere tapped his forehead. "Well, son of a bitch!" he yelled out, "son of a fucking bitch," and Dean watched every one stunned, a couple looking toward the door, as though they might exit, and not a one piping up. Would Cousin Gere pull that .45 again?

"You, and you, and you, and *you*," shouted Cousin Gere. "I did it for every one of you, and no, I ain't got the Purple Fucking Heart yet, but I will! You can count on that, chief. Maybe I'll lose a foot. Maybe a leg. An arm—both arms! But till then, I got some medals—here, you take a look. You take a fucking good long look." He shoved his chest out. Then he pointed at Dean. "*He* got any? I don't *see* any. At least dear old dad over there, he did—feast your eyes." He again pointed at Dean's father's picture on the stand. "And me, *I* do. And it ain't no chickenshit past war—it's this one, the Real War. The one that counts. The big one! And I'm making my big sacrifice so that you, and you, and you, can enjoy your fucking freedom! I'm doing it for *you*!"

At first there was a general silence, lugubrious looks all around, and then someone suddenly began clapping. Dean didn't see who it was right off, but then he saw that it was Great Uncle George, and suddenly others were clapping right along. Great Uncle Tommy with a beatific smile on his face. And then everyone was clapping, smiles enveloping their faces, except for Great Aunt Sally. She was sitting quietly, not clapping.

She was, in fact—wasn't she?—yes, tearing up. Dean saw a trickle running down her left eye. That would be her *right* eye, though, he realized from her angle of vision.

"Clap, clap, clap!" shouted Cousin Gere. "Clap all you want. But just get it through your goddamned heads what I said, and don't give me no bullshit!"

Great Uncle Tommy moved in.

"Now, now," he said. "You'd think this was a union meeting instead of a reunion! Let's enter into the bargaining stage!"

"You'd think it was an angry man with inadvisable tattooing and impaled nose, ears, or lips," said Jennifer, rising from her seat.

"You'd think it was that angry man unwilling to modify," shouted Ginger. "But . . . in this case, it's not. No, no."

"No," said Jennifer, "it's a man with a good point. Well taken, soldier!"

"We're all ears," shouted Ginger.

"Union meeting's over," said Uncle Tommy. "A new contract has been agreed upon by all parties."

"Oh, yeah?" said Cousin Gere. "Well, you're a big weapons man. You tell them."

"Hmm? Tell them what?"

"About, you know—what's *what,*" said Cousin Gere. And with Great Uncle Tommy standing before him, towering over him, he seemed somehow to relax. Dean watched him sigh even, and take his seat.

"What's what?"

Cousin Gere shifted in his seat. "Hell, why bother," he said. "What good would it do? Let bygones be bygones."

"That's the spirit, son," said Uncle Rory.

"How about a drink?" said Great Uncle Tommy.

"Affirmative," said Cousin Gere. "Just okeydokey fine."

"A good old hard drink," said Great Uncle Tommy.

"You pick it," said Cousin Gere.

"I'll do that," said Uncle Tommy, and laid a hand on Gere's shoulder.

Dean still stood by, and for a moment he looked at Jennifer. She had taken a chair and was now sitting with his mother, a bit red-eyed, the two of them talking fast. Great Aunt Sally was still wiping away a tear, and dabbing at a second streak that had slid down her other cheek. No one seemed to have noticed, except him.

Great Uncle Tommy went into the kitchen, and Dean followed, downing the rest of his beer. He went for another in the fridge.

"Been quite an event," said Great Uncle Tommy. "But is Sally there okay?" He made a gesture at her. She wasn't looking their way, though, so Dean couldn't quite tell.

"Don't know," he said.

Great Uncle Tommy clinked ice in glasses, making quite a bit of noise and began pouring from a Beam bottle. He was making two drinks. "Well, probably just the heat of the moment. Reunions can be emotional events. We'll see what we can do. Right?" He winked at Dean.

That wink. It told him, though winks didn't necessarily do this, that Great Uncle Tommy was superior to him somehow.

They left the kitchen, reentering the living room. "See how that suits, Gere," he said. He handed him one of the drinks.

Cousin Gere held the glass up in a salute, then sipped.

Dean stood by, drinking beer. He wanted to be with these men here. There was no seating room right now with Jennifer, and he wasn't much interested in good posture, or poise, or Social Graces anyway because it seemed to require too much effort—three weeks on smiling alone—and he thought they'd pretty much exhausted their possibilities for further conversation. If he could just get her good looks out of his mind, but no, he felt compelled to look her way now and then just to take her in. And then his eyes fell on Ginger. She was holding forth on something, and he wondered who looked better, Jennifer or her. Suddenly he was unable to distinguish between the two of them, the one dark-haired, the other blond. Their smiles, their gestures, looked identical. They are one and the same, he thought, trained in the Social Graces. Two Miss Manners.

"Want to know something?" said Uncle Rory to Great Uncle Tommy. "I haven't seen some of these people, like George and Sally here, for years. That's too bad, isn't it?"

"It sure is," said Great Uncle Tommy, standing by sipping his drink. "You don't want to ignore blood. You want to keep blood ties over the years, but of course now with so many broken marriages—I've had a couple myself, three, four—well, hell, that's real tough to do. It gets confusing."

"Blood's real important," said Rory.

"First it's blood, then good friends," said Tommy. "Then the rest. Well, we humans aren't too good at casting a wide net."

"What do you mean?" said Rory.

"Hard to care much, I guess," said Great Uncle Tommy. "Out of our orbit—you know? What do we know about them? Nothing, really."

"Suppose you're right," said Rory.

Dean noticed that Great Aunt Sally had begun to tear up even worse. Now a tear was actually dripping off her chin, emanating originally from her right eye—that would be *her* left, from her own angle of vision. It seemed important, Dean thought, to make this distinction because maybe which eye was involved had to do with which nerves from the brain were involved—or had he just dreamed that up? No, he was getting that from some of those brain studies Jill told him about—yes, that's where it came from. Unless he got that wrong. It was so abstruse, that stuff. But he began to worry about this elderly woman, regardless of left or right eye. She might be about to sob, and he knew, being the host of this reunion, it would fall to him to take quick action if she did. Some sort of crisis intervention might be called for. A heart attack? She looked old and feeble, ripe for one, in his opinion. He stood by, unsure, lacking confidence on how to proceed.

"You learn one thing about the world," said Great Uncle Tommy, "if you learn anything. There's the good and the bad, and we can do without the bad, can't we?"

"You learn that in my line of work for sure," said Cousin Gere.

"In ours too," said Jennifer.

"Truer words," said Ginger.

"Oh, well," said Great Uncle Tommy. "I wasn't talking line of work. I thought we'd moved beyond that. I was talking people.

Broken lines between one and others. Some you can't repair. The criminal types—as I'm sure you're aware."

"I could write the book," said Cousin Gere, "on that."

Great Aunt Sally suddenly began to speak. But she wasn't turning toward anyone, and she wasn't speaking to him, Dean. But out of her mouth was coming some sort of language, yet Dean couldn't quite make it out. A fog of guttural syllables. He leaned over to get closer, to hear better. He listened to what seemed rough notes of what she might be intending to say. He waited to hear what that was. He wanted to take in what was way down below, simmering.

Cousin Gere got an odd grin on his face. But he'd been warned by Great Uncle George, so why the distasteful grin? Dean knew this might be a prelude to a great ordeal of sobbing, and he wasn't about to grin. It wasn't in him to grin.

"What were you saying, dear?" asked Aunt Winnie, turning toward her.

Great Uncle George hurried around. He placed a hand on Dean's shoulder. "Go get a glass of water, Dean—if you would. Please hurry!"

Dean did hurry—into the kitchen, shot water into the glass, and hurried back with it. And handed it to Great Uncle George.

"Now, Sal," said Great Uncle George. "Now, now, dear." He removed a vial of pills with an orange top from his jacket pocket. He tapped one out in his palm. "This one. This one's pretty good, Sal. You know—the X-350. Better than the X-339. By far. Here's the water."

Great Aunt Sally stared off in space. And then she pushed Great Uncle George's hand away. It was not a hard push, but it was certainly a push. And when Great Uncle George said, "Sal, honey," and again brought the pill up to her lips, she once again pushed it away.

"Fear," said Cousin Gere. He bent over sniffing, his nose against the old lady's coiffured, purple hair.

Dean got up close too. "What?" he said. "What's troubling you? Is there anything I can do? Anything at all?"

Great Uncle George once again laid a hand on his shoulder. A kindly wink. Fatherly. "Not much, son, though we appreciate the effort. Don't we, Sal?"

"Is it . . . something someone said?" asked Dean.

He felt a poke. Two hard ones. "You thinking me, chief?"

Dean moved off.

"She'll be okay," said Great Uncle George. "It'll pass." He dropped the pill in the orange-lidded vial and stuck it back in his jacket. And then he grabbed the magazine he'd been looking at earlier off an empty chair. It was that same article Dean had read. The same clay-colored smudge, apparently due to the printing itself. He really hoped Great Aunt Sally hadn't seen it. But no—no, she was looking off in space somewhere, perhaps at the door. She was looking blankly at the door. Was she considering an exit?

Dean watched Great Uncle George settle back next to Ginger.

Great Uncle Tommy said, "Well, Gere, back to our subject." He nodded vigorously at Cousin Gere. "Sure, broken. The lines between one man and another, the world over—broken. *N'est-ce pas*? Everything you can name is broken. But it's always been that way. You know what the Good Book says about that. Moths, rust, etcetera. I suppose that pertains to anything here on this troubled earth—what we store up, what we are, one man to another. But we've got to do what we can. It's all we can do."

Uncle Rory held up his drink glass. "I'm about out, and ready for another. Anybody else."

"Oh, not me," said Aunt Winnie. "I've had enough. I'm getting hungry."

"After those crackers and cheese?" Uncle Rory said. He reached over and patted her stomach. "Better watch it, dear—" He rose and started for the kitchen.

"He's one to talk," shouted Aunt Winnie. "You see that mid-region of his?"

"Proud of it," said Uncle Rory, laughing, patting his potbelly. Dean heard the clinks of ice into the glass, then the pouring.

"Every goddamn thing breaks," said Gere. "You think you've got it handled, you think the assault's going to be a victory you can chalk up, but no—hell, no, the fucking bastards got you again."

"Maybe it's the age," said Uncle Rory, raising his glass.

"No, you guzzle," said Aunt Winnie.

Jennifer spoke up. "Guzzling is not good, sir."

"Bad form," said Ginger.

"Life," said Great Uncle Tommy, and Dean watched him looking over at Great Aunt Sally now.

But she wasn't saying a thing. She wasn't sobbing either, but looking straight ahead, and then she looked up at him—her eyes leveling on his, square on. For a moment, he thought he knew her, that she was someone he'd known at some other time, some other place, perhaps someone from history, some figure he couldn't quite name or place. Who, though?

"Honey," said Aunt Winnie. "There are better topics of conversation, surely—better than this. Surely."

"Affirmative," said Cousin Gere. "You're damned fucking straight on that, Mom."

"Son," said Uncle Rory, returning with his drink. "Don't talk to your mom with that kind of language. Please."

"Never happened," said Gere. "Won't happen again." He drained off his drink.

"Seems to me," said Great Uncle Tommy, "that the topic of conversation isn't the important thing. It's the good fellow feeling. And I don't know about you, but I've got a good feeling, regardless— maybe it's this drink I'm holding here, well, sure, maybe it is!—but you know what, I'm just so happy to meet every one of you. We'll all be moving on—soon, I know—but, as the English say, it's just bloody good to get to know you, each of you. And I spent some time in London, last year, and believe me, they don't have what we have here. No one does. Not on the face of the earth. In my opinion, at least."

"Fucking A," said Cousin Gere. "And they got bombed all to hell in the Second One. You got to hand them that. Europe too. Keep it over there is all I say. You don't fucking want it over here."

"Pardon your French, son," said Rory.

And Dean wondered: he waits until now to say this?

"Yeah?" said Gere.

"Yes, sir, son," said Rory.

"Don't call me sir!"

"Never happened," said Uncle Rory.

"Well, that's a good sentiment indeed to have," said Great Uncle Tommy. "Indeed it is."

Great Aunt Sally, now letting out a choking sobbing sound, suddenly cried out: "I've seen it!" And then there was that Latin or something that followed, burbling out of her mouth—because Dean himself couldn't follow it. Had she heard that in Mass, perhaps?

Great Uncle Tommy reached down to touch her on the shoulder. He gave her a couple pats. "I'm sorry if we've upset you," he said. "You can be sure we didn't mean to."

She said nothing for a moment, and then she said in a low, grave voice. "I've seen it."

"I know you have."

"First death, then the judgment," she said quietly.

"Hmm?" said Great Uncle Tommy.

"Esoteric," said Jennifer.

"Perhaps she needs a facial," said Ginger. "You know if you go too long on a thing like that—"

"Gets one twice a month," said Great Uncle George.

"Commendable. A regular schedule is important," said Ginger.

She's in a trance, thought Dean. Now and then, she goes into a trance. He wanted to understand it. He wanted to study each nuance of it.

He went to her, leaned over, and patted her shoulder. Her shoulder was bony, and he wondered how much flesh she had on her body. She seemed so slight, so frail. And he hoped it wouldn't come down to a 911 call.

Great Uncle George arrived. "Is there something the matter, dear?" he asked.

Another burbling sound came out of her throat. Her eyes looked glassy, feverish, and they danced around. No words appeared to be forthcoming.

Trance, yes.

"Well, let's change the subject, shall we?" said Great Uncle George, chipper. "Probably something's been upsetting Sal, but we'll move on to something else. Okay, folks?"

"Upsetting her?" said Cousin Gere. "First we got some dipwad who writes about it, then we've got this dipwad's mother who thinks she knows all about the fucking war, and the super fucking Purple Heart, then we've got this old broad sitting here croaking over it. Give me a fucking break! Will the whole goddamned world just give me one big fucking break!"

"Wait a minute!" said Great Uncle George. "Old broad?"

"Fucking A. If the shoe fits—"

"I take exception," said Great Uncle George. "I take exception to that, Gere."

"The fuck you say."

"Pardon your French!" shouted Rory. But that mischievous grin followed. He patted Gere on the shoulder.

"That *language*," said Great Uncle George, shaking his head. "Really, Gere, you should watch that, especially in mixed company—"

"Son," said Uncle Rory. "Son, son."

"I think we'd better leave," said Aunt Winnie. "I think we'd just better leave. I'm so embarrassed. I'm just petrified."

"It's all gone so, so bad!" cried Dean's mother. "And I tried so hard! We cleaned. We straightened. We washed, mopped, dusted! Me! Dean too!"

"Now, now," said Jennifer.

"Emotion is good," said Ginger. "Let it out, dear. Let it all out."

And now Dean felt wrongly accused. *Writes* about it? He had hardly written an f-ing word. He had hardly settled on a topic. He must confront Cousin Gere on this fact. He raised a finger, wiggling it a little. "I've not written anything, really. And you see, this is the problem—"

"Yeah, chief?"

"But you're working at it, aren't you?" said Great Uncle Tommy. "And I think right now, before we proceed any further, let's all get a free breath of air, clean the old slate, and help Dean solve his problem. What better thing to do for blood kin than help them get their master's degree! What do you all say? We've got some educated people in this room, so what do you all say?"

They began to clap, clap, clap, clap, and Dean felt embarrassed, with all eyes focused on him, as though he were about to give a speech or play a part.

"Dean?" said Great Uncle Tommy. "Brainstorm it. What'll it be?"

"Yeah, chief," said Cousin Gere. "What'll it be?"

"Give the man a moment to answer," said Great Uncle George. "And maybe a hard drink or two!"

From her chair, Ginger raised a champagne flute and yelled, "Hurrah!"

"Well, I did think of one thing," said Dean, spirited now. But then he noticed Great Aunt Sally, who had once again leveled her eyes on his. She seemed to know him, and him her. In a way that others didn't. She knew his interior. She knew what was in him and what wasn't. It frightened him. Or rather deadened him in the gut. And yet—and yet, he felt compelled to speak.

And so he did: "Maybe," said Dean, "Maybe I'll deal with . . . war criminals—with the way they behave when charged . . . I've been kicking that around"—why had he just said that? For one thing, it wasn't true. He'd just come up with it on the spot. And to put it that way—why? Nerves. But he went on, his face flushing hot: "*Miss Manners for War Criminals*—I'll call it that."

Where had that come from?

He saw the inquisitive eyes of Jennifer. Of Ginger. Had he misspoken? But there it was, he'd said what he'd said, and probably they had influenced him. It had all been working in his brain, and he hadn't even been aware of it. That's the way it was, said those neuroscientists.

"That does put an interesting spin on the matter," said Great Uncle Tommy. "Good job!"

"War criminals. Damn straight," said Cousin Gere. "You do that, chief, and you got my respect. Because there's plenty of them to go around. Fucking guys don't care about their own lives, but don't have to take me with them—huh? Do they?"

Great Uncle Tommy laughed. "Well, I'll tell you what I'd do, Dean, if I were a war criminal—so-charged, I mean. I'd deny it all. You couldn't drag it out of me. And I'd be following the etiquette laid out by Miss Manners all right because the worst thing you can do is get all tight-assed, pardon *my* French. The war criminals in history we do know about were tricky little devils, and that's the way to go, is all I'm saying. Be polite. Be polished. Present thyself well! Oh, but I'm not saying to *be* a war criminal, I'm not saying that at all, for heaven's sake, but I *am* saying if you're caught with the goods, it comes down to defending yourself. Plain and simple. You've got a right to it—fight or flight. That's primal in us. If they're going to hang you out to dry, well, you've got a right to use all your wiles to save your own skin. Right?"

"Um," said Dean.

He suddenly looked at Great Aunt Sally, now slumped toward the floor. He imagined Jennifer would have some recommendations for her, posture-wise. Though maybe she was too old, too bony, for that kind of thing to take effect or make much difference, one way or the other.

Aunt Winnie was looking at her. "I just feel so bad all of a sudden," she said.

"You now?" said Uncle Rory. "Why?"

"Oh, it's been one thing after another. One thing after another."

"Mom," said Cousin Gere. "Maybe I shoot my mouth off too much, but damn it I just ask for a little respect. For what I do."

Aunt Winnie leaned over toward him. "Has there ever been a time, honey—"

"He's got a point," jumped in Uncle Rory. "We *all* want respect for what we do. And some of our brave men and women in uniform don't get that respect—respect that's certainly due them."

"Affirmative," said Gere.

"Well, we'll see about that later today, won't we, Jean?"

"Yes, sir," she answered tearfully.

"We'll see about respect a bit later," said Great Uncle Tommy. "You bet."

"What?" said Gere.

"Just wait, sir."

"Goddamn it, don't call me sir, Tommy."

"Oh, sorry . . . but anyway, for now . . . sometimes at those union meetings, I don't feel I get a lot of respect, you know, so I know what Gere means by respect," said Great Uncle Tommy. "I suppose I didn't have a lot of that myself as a young man—no offense, Gere. I'm speaking of myself now. Back then, I was sort of scattered, loose, ragtag, uncommitted on the whole. Didn't have much respect for myself—or my work. Or anything—I guess you could say—of value. Today, though, that plant I run, that division of the plant, I mean—well, I can't be that way. It's up and at 'em, as my sainted father used to say. Each and every day a new problem to solve, and you've got to get it right, no errors permitted, no slacking, because they're counting on you, men like Gere here. And when the war began, I knew it would be get-it-in-gear time. When we launched those first strikes, burned that damned city . . . and then the ones after that . . . well, you know, pretty well obliterated several other cities, well, we used our stock of fireworks up . . . so, I knew we'd have to go double, hell, triple time to get the job done. And you don't think that put a strain on a man's life? Aggravated the ulcers? I was having to go nearly round the clock trying to meet deadlines. It was one thing or another they needed, and they needed it right now. They needed a whole new arsenal of our best—you see? That takes time. But do you have the time?"

"You fucking A," said Cousin Gere.

"You know how long it takes to teach good posture?" said Jennifer.

"Both sitting and standing—and walking?" said Ginger.

"I can imagine," said Great Uncle Tommy. "But anyway, where I was going . . . you don't replenish your whole fireworks assortment over night, you know."

"And you don't talk your way out of it if you come up short-handed," said Cousin Gere.

"I'll bet you don't. That's absolutely right!" said Great Uncle Tommy, smiling.

"What's wrong, Sal?" asked Aunt Winnie.

She still said nothing. But her eyes were studied, her lips frozen solid. She looked half dead or near it. A drink. Maybe a drink. "Would you like a drink?" Dean asked her.

No response.

"Would you?" he asked.

Great Uncle George massaged his shoulder.

"I could go for another drink," he said, looking at Great Aunt Sally. "Anybody else?"

"No—not me."

"Fine here."

"Me too. Fine."

Uncle Rory said to Dean: "You ought to talk to Gere about that thesis. Since he's in the biz. I'll bet you, I'll just bet you, he'd have some ideas. Some real corkers!"

"Hmm," said Dean. He looked at Cousin Gere.

Cousin Gere grinned. "Yeah, I could fill your ears but good, bud. If you'd pay me the respect to listen. That's all I ask. Pay me that respect."

Dean nodded. "Sure," he said. Because how could he say no to a man like Cousin Gere? He did not want to set him off.

Cousin Gere said they should go outside, down on the sidewalk, way out of earshot of Great Aunt Sally—he didn't need that old broad running her yap.

"Um," said Dean.

So they did.

Five minutes later, Cousin Gere was leaning up against the building smoking, saying "*Ah*—finally. Son of a bitch." And then he began to flick ashes and steady his eyes on Dean. When Dean said he could sure use a notebook, "Just wait a minute," and started to go, Cousin Gere grabbed his wrist, gripping it savagely, setting Dean's skin on fire. "Don't take notes," he said. "Just lean your ears this way. Huh, chief? Lean your ears this way."

PART TWO
THE SOFT-SHOE

1

"Now, folks, I've got a bit of a surprise—remember about later, and that business of respect I mentioned?" Great Uncle Tommy said, turning to Gere.

"Yeah, yeah."

The large man held a ballpoint pen poised above a notepad. "I'm treating everyone to supper at The Soft-Shoe. Have you been there? They've got truly scrumptious food there, I can assure you. And you'll not be starved for recreation or entertainment—they've also got a dance floor! And . . . now hear this: tonight is a *special* night—a fundraiser for our troops night! Guess who's involved in the festivities."

Dean started to say, but Great Uncle Tommy clicked his ballpoint and shouted out: "Jennifer and Ginger, our very own! With a dance number! Isn't that right?"

They were nodding and blushing.

A round of clapping. Loud yells from the men, and *ooohs* from the women—even Jennifer and Ginger, well, except for Great Aunt Sally. There was a zombie look on her face that Dean wanted to decipher. He wanted to puzzle it out closely. He wanted to ask a neurologist for some sort of clinical analysis. A work-up of some kind.

"Maybe they'll teach us how to dance and prance!" shouted out Great Uncle Tommy. "Do you think?"

"Gere?" said Great Uncle George.

"Whoop Dee Doo!" shouted Cousin Gere.

"Do you dance, Gere?" asked Tommy.

Cousin Gere raised his glass. "I make'm dance, you bet. To my tune."

"Well, then maybe you can show us how!"

"Be real pleased," said Cousin Gere, only Dean thought the Marine suddenly grew morose. He nursed his drink. Maybe it was that one-hour face-to-face on war and what Cousin Gere called "doing what you fucking A well better do, chief" that made him that way. Dean's ears were still burning at some of the images rattling in his brain.

"When's this supper thing going to occur?" asked Aunt Winnie. "I'm starved."

Uncle Rory turned and pointed at her. "This woman—you can't fill her up. I'll bet she eats every minute of the day. I swear."

Aunt Winnie jabbed a finger into Uncle Rory's paunch. "As I've said before, he's one to talk."

Uncle Rory roared: "Well, I'm hungry too, and I don't much care about this gut-o-mine. When's the big doings, Tommy?"

"How about," said Great Uncle Tommy, "we all meet out there at the Soft-Shoe about six? Jean?"

"Yes!" she exclaimed. "Great idea!"

"They've got some real great specials out there," said Great Uncle Tommy. "But you're going to have to pay for those yourself— just wanted to caution you. They've got barnacles . . . yes, barnacles, a *delicacy*, indeed. And you won't have to hang off the side of the ship in dry dock. They'll bring them right to your table! And fried worms, if you go for that. And, listen up: very popular in Asia— bird nests! Now . . . if you want to go for any of these fine foods— these delicacies—folks, that's definitely your prerogative, but I ain't a-paying for it! But I *am* paying for anything else you order. Earth to reunion people: Got that one?"

A general buzz of "Yes!" and a round of clapping followed.

"Great!" shouted Great Uncle Tommy. "You're my guests then— with that one proviso on those particular food groups."

More clapping, and more "Yes!" Most of it from the two young women, Jennifer and Ginger.

"Now! I'd like to say one additional thing," said Great Uncle Tommy, with a sly grin. "In that the Soft-Shoe thinks highly enough of our two gals here to hire them for their fundraising festivities tonight, and by virtue of the fact that they *are* experts in the Art of Social Graces, I'll just bet you dollars to donuts they know something about taking a crew of this size out there to the Soft-Shoe and showing them one hell of a fine time! The best possible purchase for their money!"

"Money," said Gere.

"Oh . . . doesn't apply—in this case, Gere! But what do you all think—just give our two gals a look. I myself vote to have them in charge of this family reunion's night-time festivities. Do I have a second on that?"

A shout of "Yes!" from Great Uncle George.

"You've got a third on that one!" yelled Uncle Rory, rising from the sofa.

"All right, then! Are you two very special women ready to put on the mantle?" asked Great Uncle Tommy, leaning toward them, clicking his ballpoint. It looked to Dean as though he were an entertainer and was at the mic, beckoning them forward.

"Jen?" said Ginger.

Jen smiled, nodded

Ginger stood up. "Indeed we *will*, Tommy—indeed we will be very happy to put on the mantle. But *first*"—and Ginger now turned to the whole group, her eyes scanning them like a video cam—"and I mean no offense now. So please, please, don't take it that way. But see, part of my profession is to be right out there with it—not to . . . what they call wimp it!" She laughed. "Forthrightness—right, Jen?"

"That's right!"

"Well, okay, then, keeping that in mind, as to my best intentions for each and every one here, I've witnessed a couple of explosions. And after all, tempers do run high at reunions, as has been my experience. So, given that fact about the human animal in proximity to other such human animals—and that's our specialty, isn't it, Jen: the human animal?"

"Indeed it is," said Jen.

"Well, given that fact, I'd like to suggest that there are certain topics suitable for reunions, while other topics are just *not* as suitable for reunions. I'm not ruling them out . . . but they're just not as . . . suitable. Did I hesitate? Well, all right I hesitated! But you see, it comes down to survival skills, and that gets back to *appropriateness*. At a reunion, nothing that smacks of anything very serious at all is appropriate. Me, I'd like to talk about feminist issues—oh, do believe me, I just surely would!" She laughed loud, a brazen booming, but somehow so graciously, Dean thought, and so gracefully. "Me, I'd like to talk about woman-haters that have smashed the woman and her body for millennia, but do you think I'm going to have it out with each and every one of you here over that—no, I'm not!" She laughed again—a quick one.

"Nor I!" shouted Jennifer.

"What then?" asked Ginger. "Short answer: I'm saying that if we're all a-herding out to the Soft-Shoe, with the purpose of re-*creating*—that's what recreation means, you know—Jen?"

"Absolutely!"

"Well, let's just do that. Is everybody with me?"

Great Uncle Tommy shouted out: "Great ideas, Ginger, every single one of them! That's what happens when the women take charge!" He did a kind of soft-shoe, with several easeful steps, and Dean thought that a man with Great Uncle Tommy's poise could do that, but he himself would look rather foolish.

Dean saw that Cousin Gere was looking off in space, rubbing a finger over the rim of his drink glass. He tried to judge the expression on his face. Grim, wasn't it? Was it anger? Outrage? Was another explosion about to occur?

And what about Great Aunt Sally? She too was staring off in space. But she looked blank. Or *was* that blank? Was there something underneath it? Yes, he thought, there was. He was sure he detected anguish. He was sure he saw it in the smile lines of her face, which, it was clear to see, were greenish gray. A look of mortality. A look of descending, sinking—the woman could go any moment. He couldn't even imagine her standing up. Was it in her to rise, to go vertical? Perhaps she would sit there forever. The brain was the engine of every movement in the body, according to the neurologists, and so here she was totally slack. The engine was dead, as was she.

More hearty shouts akin to Great Uncle Tommy's, especially from Great Uncle George and Uncle Rory, but then Aunt Winnie yelled out: "It's about time the women took charge!" She swung her glass, partially filled with golden liquid, above her head.

"Mother," said Cousin Gere. "Hell . . . well, hell why not?" He glugged down his hard drink.

"That's the spirit, son," said Uncle Rory and whacked him on the back.

Cousin Gere sputtered. "Damn, Dad."

"Sorry, son."

"Amen to that!" shouted Dean's mother, and then put her hand up to her mouth, embarrassed. Was his mother hitting the stiff stuff? Too hard? Dean watched.

Great Uncle George was moving toward her. "A smashing good time we've had!"

"Oh, George!" she cried out, and she took a quick sip from her drink glass. It was amber. It was that Beam of a certainty.

2

There they were, finally, at about six o'clock, Jill with him after he'd pleaded with her to show up, catching a whine in his voice, saying how Great Uncle Tommy, the one that ran the weapons plant, or a division of it anyway, and had plenty of dough, was springing for a free meal—and then special entertainment to follow. Dancing.

He could rake himself over the coals, he thought, for that *springing* business. And then he wanted to rake himself over the coals for even thinking *rake myself over the coals*, damn it! Emerson was right, he thought, so long ago. The deterioration of the language! Now, though, everything was one big cliché! Hollow words! Meaningless! But when he'd protested to Jill about this continual tapestry of clichés woven into nearly every aspect of the culture, into his and everyone else's constant conversation, she had said: "Maybe *you're* a cliché."

"Huh? Me?" He was immediately offended.

"How do you know you're not?"

"I try not to be."

"Keep trying," she said.

"What?"

"No one," she told him, "can escape being a cliché. That's who we are. We're a repeat of everything that came before us, and everything that follows will be a repeat of us. The good and the bad."

"No," he said. "No, no."

"It's true. Depressing, isn't it?"

"That sounds deterministic," he said. "I thought we had free will."

She stared at him, silent.

"I hope we have," he said.

"Even so," she said.

It didn't add up, but he put it to rest.

Jill said she was hungry, being low on groceries, so okay, she'd show up. But she didn't know about the entertainment. Dancing?

No . . . . She was pretty busy with several articles that were clinchers, she thought, on defeating behaviorist thinking. And a few more books too, and she hoped this wouldn't take all night. Perhaps they could be out of there in a few hours? Or at least she could? "I do, you know, have a paper due on Monday."

He had no idea. He could promise nothing. After all, he was co-hosting, in a way, as the man of the family, and he imagined his mother wouldn't want him to leave her holding the bag. Oh, hell, he thought. Damn! Another f-ing cliché! And a particularly bad one—old, crusted over . . . . Which were the worst, the old or the newly hatched? But he realized he was losing track, and so he contemplated the matter. This supper thing, it was after all Great Uncle Tommy's treat, and Ginger and Jennifer were in charge of running the show—a literal show, and so no cliché. At least he wasn't co-hosting. But still, if he suddenly left, there would be the problem of impoliteness, the matter of Social Graces—wouldn't there be?

Red, white, and blue banners were strung across the ceiling of the Soft-Shoe's huge dance floor announcing:

FUNDRAISER FOR THE TROOPS!

SUPPORT OUR BRAVE MEN AND WOMEN IN UNIFORM!

GIVE TILL IT HURTS!

The place had an eerie atmosphere, Dean thought, with the silky white curtains billowing against the walls like they were being puffed by the April breezes. But perhaps this was from air conditioner vents.

There was a jazz band playing loud and shrill.

They sat at a long table, with steak and baked potatoes before them, and salad, with beer or wine. Dessert was apple pie. Great Uncle Tommy sat to Dean's left side, Jill to his right, and directly across from them was Cousin Gere, then four places to Gere's right were marked "Guest Dancers." At the opposite end of the table were gathered Dean's mother, Great Uncle George, Great Aunt Sally, Uncle Rory and Aunt Winnie. Jennifer and Ginger were seated across from each other at the very end of the table. They would soon, Dean imagined, be popping up to take their lead, but right now they were eating, regularly dabbing their lips with a crimson colored cloth napkin.

Dean had ignored his steak, as had Jill, both vegetarians.

"Ugh," whispered Jill, "flesh."

"Nice napkins, though, aren't they?" he whispered to Jill.

"Perfect," she said. Her eyes were on Jennifer and Ginger. She'd been introduced by Dean's mother before they sat down, and she hadn't said much. Other than: "They're a couple of sweeties, aren't they—those two young women?"

"I suppose," he had said.

Now she said, "My, my, how many times are those women going to dab their lips with their napkins?"

"Whatever it takes, I guess," said Dean.

"That Jennifer. I'll bet you find her sensual, seductive, don't you?" She was whispering, but not low enough, apparently, and Gere must have heard.

"Yeah, yeah," he said. "So you're Dean's woman. That it?"

Jill took umbrage. "I am my own woman."

"Yeah, yeah," he said.

Dean felt his knee being gripped. He was to defend Jill's honor.

"Look here," he said.

"What?"

"Look here."

"Yeah, chief?"

"Leave her alone. You hear me?"

Gere smirked. "Now what did I do?"

Jill squeezed his knee harder.

"You better fucking not bother her!" Dean came back. And with force. This was not an athletic frat jock, but even worse, a hired killer—a damned f-ing Marine!

"Yeah, yeah," said Gere. "Yeah, yeah."

Dean suddenly wished they'd mix it up. He wanted it. He greatly desired it.

He felt a pat on his knee. Jill leaned toward him and kissed him.

"My, my," said Uncle Rory. "We caught that. Public displays of affection! PDA!"

"I think it's sweet," said Aunt Winnie.

"Young people," rang out Great Uncle George.

He felt Great Uncle Tommy's pat on the back.

Cousin Gere sneered.

"Well," said Dean's mother. She raised her napkin to her lips, her eyes on Jill. Was that a scowl?

His mother had been short with Jill, as usual, and now she was staring at her for some reason. Dean leaned toward that end of the table. "What, Mother?" he said.

"I hope you are enjoying yourself," she said. "But Jill doesn't look like she is."

"I am here," said Jill. "I am eating."

"I suppose that's all my son can expect," said Dean's mother.

Dean gave it up. His mother would never accept Jill, his sultry lover. Smart, beautiful. The smart part was the bad part for his mother.

He turned his attention to a menu loose on the table in front of him. He held it up.

"Chief?" said Gere. He motioned.

He handed it to Cousin Gere, who scanned it for a moment or two. "Get this, hombre," he said. "One hundred bucks for the barnacles. Two hundred a pop for the fried fucking worms. Five thousand for the goddamned bird nests! Hell," he shouted, "I'll chip off my own, dig them with a spade, grab them off a tree!"

The band was now playing softer. Music meant for gracious gliding.

Couples soon covered nearly a third of the huge dance floor in the middle. Now and then certain couples seemed to dominate the floor, with other couples stopping, watching, and applauding—apparently celebrating those with the most flair. Dean was particularly impressed with some of the tricky movements he saw, some of the footwork, and the posture of those who glided almost, not exactly danced—at least from what he was seeing.

Meanwhile he was ruminating on all the things Cousin Gere had said about war, which he'd been able to place in three basic categories: *Attack*, *Reconnaissance*, and *Patrol*. They had stood outside the apartment, on the sidewalk, with Cousin Gere kicking the building as he smoked and spoke. "You fuckin' A do *whatever* to stop the Bad Asses, Dean. Fuckin' A. You keep in mind, hoss, who you're dealin' with, your first-rate, top-of-the-line, Mother-fucking Insurgent Bad Asses!" Dean recalled particular images of bloody, mangled bodies, torturing—"Yeah, we torture, hell yeah . . . I getta chance, I'll up it, chief. Huh? Up it so you can't fuckin' believe it. You got a prob with that, Dean-o boy? Huh?" And he thrust a finger against Dean's chest. Thrust, thrust, thrust. Hard, harder, hardest. It hurt. Bad.

Now as he sat watching the proceedings at the Soft-Shoe, Dean couldn't help but reflect on those images: dark, grisly, meat bloody. Freddy Krueger, he thought. Yeah.

"I don't know these people at all," whispered Jill. "I don't understand at all why I'm here."

"Free food?"

"Well," she said. "And a slab of meat that totally endears me."

My mother wishes you weren't here, he wanted to say, but didn't. She knew that already.

As they ate, Dean glanced now and then at Cousin Gere, but he had his head down as he cut with his steak knife, then forked, then shoveled in the bright red meat. Eventually, Jennifer and Ginger stood up, and Ginger began tinging a spoon on a saucer. Then she put down both spoon and saucer and took her napkin and again wiped her mouth carefully as she cleared her throat and began to speak.

"Jen and I are up soon for the Jen and Gin Dance Team Show— you'll hear the announcement anytime now! And we want to invite *you*—and your very own blood relatives—to get involved. So what do you say?"

There was some hesitation, some "Um, don't know about that," but then Great Uncle Tommy rose from the table and said, "Sure—

you bet! No party poops here!" He sat back down.

And Uncle Rory yelled out, "Get a man drunk enough, he'll do anything!" Then a hearty round of "Okay!" and some clapping, and Ginger shouted, "Great!" and went on: "And now, Jennifer and I will split up our roles in the festivities. Jennifer's going to be in charge of the Social Graces—physical-wise. I will head up the more behavioral aspects of the Art and Practice. If that's okay with Jen, who's the Master Worker of the Smile!"

"That's A-*okay* with me," said Jen, smiling.

"Okeydoke! Now—since we're truly in charge ... of the festivities ... you will please allow us two professional gals to actually *run* this show—according to our professional judgment. Because you men, you've run the show long enough, now haven't you?"

Dean's eyes fell on Cousin Gere, and he saw a sly smirk on his face, and then noted a kind of growl being emitted from his lips. Great Uncle Tommy must have seen it too because he said, "Be a good sport there, Gere. It's all in fun."

"Not like we haven't given them Every Chance," said Cousin Gere, "Over Here and Over There, and some of them have proved Every Bit as Good as the Men. I give them that."

Dean couldn't help but hear the capitalizations. Cousin Gere was somehow steeped in them.

Jill whispered at him. "I'm not dancing—no way. So don't get any ideas." She was working on her apple pie now, and Dean feared her suddenly wiping her mouth, then taking off. Leaving this whole thing to him, this dancing thing. He wasn't one to do it. He didn't have it in him.

"I suppose some people think it's fun," he said.

Jill whispered louder. "Now, Dean, listen. No. You *hear* me. I'm not going to be made a fool of. By those Two Silly Women There." She didn't point, but he was sure he heard the capitalizations.

"Now, Rec-rea-tors!" shouted out Ginger. "You see those people on the Soft-Shoe polished floor? Winging around in each other's arms? Behold them! They hain't exactly doing the soft-shoe, is they?"

They all watched as the dancers seemed to float over the polished floor, like swans on the surface of a lake, the band greasing, it seemed, their ability to glide.

Dean wondered: were they professionals? They did seem to be making all the right dance steps. Intricate, easeful movements. Maybe it was the polish of the floor, such a wonderful bright brown sheen, but then the Soft-Shoe was no slouch of a place either, and he thought you had a right to expect shiny, polished hardwood for a dance floor in an expensive place like this. He'd seen the price on the menu: $1000 a plate. Fundraiser price, of course. But he'd heard the regular price at this place was rather steep anyway and certainly over his budget. Great Uncle Tommy was indeed sparing nothing. Well, except for those delicacies. Did he get some sort of break for bringing in so many diners? One thousand a whack. The troops were certainly getting supported. Tommy was giving till it hurt!

"Hurrah!" shouted out Ginger, making a sweeping gesture at the dancers. "Aren't they just wonderful? Our team has got some tough competition, *n'est-ce pas*? But we'll give them a Run for Their Money!"

His own dancing skills were to be abhorred, he knew, but Jill, if she would only participate, had remarkable grace, and he would love to see her in Jen's hands, exhibiting this grace for everyone here to behold. Ah yes, true grace. Lithe, lively—such, what? Sex. Yes, such sex, he knew it to be true.

"Now, now, now!" shouted out Ginger. "Hark ye! It's Recruiting Time. Oyez, oyez—Recruiting Time. We've got only a few minutes before the Show starts!" And she let out a big, hearty, brassy laugh. "Yes, it's time for our first participant. I won't call him—yes, *men*, I mean *you*—a victim. Just our first man to come up and let Two Gals Who know What They're Doing Do Their Thing."

Suddenly Great Uncle Tommy rose from his chair and marched forward like a new convert to the faith, but not to the altar—no, to the dance floor, which was just beyond their table, not more than ten feet off, like a skating rink where they would soon begin to skate off, but would it be effortlessly? Dean doubted that, given Great Uncle Tommy's advanced age.

The dancers still glided across the floor, elegantly dressed.

The band seemed to oil their dance shoes.

Dean felt out of order in his black slacks, sport coat, and cheap brown tie. At least it wasn't Tuxedo Time in his own quarter.

Great Uncle Tommy stood with the two girls, and then gave them each a hug. Poise. He had great poise. And that smile, so natural, so winning.

"Wonderful!" shouted out Ginger. "But we could sure use another man up here. A Man—yes. And don't be so tied to your male-role behaviors that you can't, like some do in other cultures, dance with another man. Do you *always* have to dance with a woman? Yes, yes, yes, that's what we see out there on yon floor"— and she pointed, and again there was the veritable whirlwind of dancing legs, smoothly circling the floor, perhaps even *above* the floor, man with woman, the highly polished hardwood of the Soft-Shoe, though this clearly *wasn't* soft-shoe.

"She's right," shouted out Jennifer, whose voice was much higher, richer, wonderfully soprano. "Ginger's spot-on as far as that goes. Break the mold! Break with your cultural barriers for a minute to take a dance step with your brother—may I put it that way, Gin?"

"You most certainly may, Jen," said Ginger, laughing, again in that brassy, brazen way she had, but suddenly gravel coming at the end, as though it were some sort of crunchy rock bed underneath it all. "Brother, comrade, pal, fraternal order of the ... oh, what the hell! ... anyway, you get the point. Only just get rid of those lines, those straight lines, those fences, those stiff rectangular shapes— see what Jen and I mean?"

"You mean to change us!" shouted out Uncle Rory, laughing—or rather, Dean thought, hooting.

"Indeed no!" shouted out Ginger. "To simply *Rec*-reate you. Not to *Re*-create you, dear! Only *you* can do that!" She cupped her hands like a megaphone: "Though some might wish it!"

"Oh, my, my, my!" yelled Dean's mother. "She's a wit! Ginger, Ginger, Ginger! She's a wit!"

Jill was again whispering in his ear. "Your mother is so—damn!"

Gere saw this. "Hey, hombre, you going up there. Give them a demo?"

"No," said Dean.

"Dance and prance?" said Gere.

"Where do you and your kind come from?" said Jill. She was actually pointing at him.

"A place you'll never go," said Gere.

"Jean, I'll take that for a compliment," said Ginger. "But who's our second victim—or rather participant?"

Dean would never have imagined it, but Cousin Gere now stood up, pushed back his chair, and headed straight for them. And once there, he said nothing, just stood there, and let both Jen and Ginger give him a big hug. And now he was going to dance? With Great Uncle Tommy? No, Dean wouldn't have it. No, they'd end up dancing with Jennifer and Ginger, probably, and then Dean feared something. What if he himself felt propelled to the floor? What if he ended up dancing with Jennifer, or Ginger? What about that buzz in his groin, and then Jill—seated right here—she'd see it. Or sense it. Wouldn't she?

Or god no, what if he ended up dancing with Gere? With a Marine? In that full-dress uniform of his—with all those medals?

But no, apparently that was nothing to be concerned about, on either front, because Ginger was now arranging Great Uncle Tommy and Cousin Gere in a sort of line. A line of two? This appeared to be a Greek sort of dance or something, and then it struck Dean that Cousin Gere, with his overseas experience, probably had picked up the dances of other cultures. But which ones? One must watch for steps, different ones—perhaps he would spin around.

Suddenly there was loud static, then a voice clearing, from way across the dance floor. A man in a black suit and bright red tie leaned forward at a mic: "Folks, folks, folks! I hope you're enjoying the great food here tonight. The wonderful, delicious, scrumptious, tasty . . should I go on? . . . delectable food! And . . . Our Three Delicacies! And . . . as you know"—he pointed up at the red, white, and blue banners strung across the ceiling—"it's Fundraising Night for the Troops. For our Brave Men and Women in Uniform. And now, in that regard, we have some lively entertainment in store. Several acts. Dances, mimes, this, that—the other. But first off, we will rock on to the Jen and Gin Dance Team Show! They'll be coming around and recruiting from the tables—and it might just be *yours*!—while you finish your desserts. Meanwhile, while they get their act together . . . hmmm?" A laugh. A kind of snort. And rolling laughter from the sea of tables. "Well . . . meanwhile, enjoy your last morsels—and the *regular* dancing! Dance all you want—until Gin and Jen take the floor!"

Saxes wailed. Trumpets honked.

"Dominatrix!" shouted someone.

"Who said that?" said the man at the mic, but he laughed.

"Women ruling over us!" shouted another man.

"Brave women!" shouted the man at the mic.

And a large clapping began. It didn't die down until the man at the mic shouted, and shouted, then static filling the Soft-Shoe. Then a quiet descended on them. A hush of immense proportions.

"Like a tomb in here," said Jill.

And then the man at the mic pointed their way. "Gin and Jen!"

Ginger and Jennifer took a bow. Gracious, they looked.

There was mighty applause from the sea of tables. A real clap-off. The clapping died, finally, and Ginger grabbed a mic close by and let out a yell: "You heard the man! We've got our marching orders!"

A round of clapping and hooting.

And then Ginger leaned in toward Cousin Gere and whispered something at him.

He stood there, perplexed looking.

She whispered again.

He stood there, perplexed.

"Please," she said. Aloud.

He nodded. He smirked.

And then Ginger signaled Jennifer.

"Let's go nab them!" shouted Ginger at the mic. And Dean watched the two women hurry off, running/skipping across the dance floor, then slowing their steps as they made their way around the periphery, from table to table. He watched some shaking of heads, some abashed looks, some riotous movement of hands waving them away, but then he heard Ginger's raucous voice, aubible even from a distance: "Any sports fans around here? *Whoa*. . . Football! Soccer? *Ummm*. What! Big Game Hunting? Canned Big Game—really?"

The two women soon disappeared into the sea of tables.

Jill said, "I really don't see much to this. I mean, come on. Why do I want to watch a bunch of people up there making fools of themselves? Do they even know how to dance?" She pointed at Great Uncle Tommy and Cousin Gere, standing by. "I mean if they *do*, sure, that might be something to behold, but if they're just going to prance around, well, then I've got work to do. And so do you."

"Reunion," he said. "I'm sort of stuck."

"Yeah? But this?"

Dean's eyes traveled first to where Jennifer and Ginger went and then to Great Uncle Tommy and Cousin Gere. They were inching closer and closer now to the dance floor, as though about to try out a few tentative dance steps.

The table suddenly roared, and Dean saw why. Ginger and Jennifer had in tow four men, all middle-aged, who were hurry-walking along on the edge of the dance floor in what appeared to be an effort to get to this shindig as fast as they could. They looked utterly delighted to be part of it all.

There was laughing at the many tables, and *rah rahs*, and applause. And then the people went back to eating, talking, drinking. And dancing or floating—which was it?—on the shimmering floor. He couldn't see their feet touch it. They seemed to be about an inch or two off the floor.

"Let me introduce!" shouted out Ginger to the reunion table.

"Let me introduce my new friends as soon as I catch my breath—and as soon as they catch *theirs*. Before we get on stage—before we take that floor!" She gave it a general wave. And yelled, "Rah! Rah!"

"Amen to that," said one of them. The others shouted out, "Amen, brother," and "You got it!" and "Let's go for it!" They nodded their heads and grinned with rows of white teeth, polished, straightened. Well-heeled, thought Dean. Those suits they wore, blue, brown, black—silk maybe?

"Now," said Ginger, "the old guard you just joined, men, are Mr. Gumm, a weapons manufacturer, and Mr. Packall, a Marine—as you see. *Your* names, please! Last names only now . . . with the *Mr.* added. We will respect your right to *that* as long as we don't know you on a first-name basis—politeness and decorum, you see! Isn't that right, Jen?"

"Yes, indeed!"

"Last names and professions! A man is known by what he *does*—I can't help it, gents, it's just true. We're working on it, we women!"

Jen shouted out, "Bravo!"

A round of hoots. Clapping.

"You, sir—first," Ginger said to a man in a blue suit.

"Mr. Dollar. *Banker.* Now, listen, folks I can't help it, that's my family name, and so don't blame me—please!"

Laughter from the table, from the line of men. Clapping. Dean found himself clapping too, and then he stopped once he caught Jill's indignant expression.

"Why," she whispered, "am I *here*?"

"We won't laugh," Ginger shouted out. "I assure you. Because I once knew a dentist named Doctor Drill, I kid you not. Next!"

A loud yell from Uncle Rory: "I can tell you worse!"

"Don't!" shouted Ginger.

"Mr. Armour. Federal court judge!"

"Get out of here!" yelled Ginger and placed a hand on his shoulder. "I grabbed a *federal court judge* over there"—she pointed in the direction of the tables across the dance floor. "Next!"

"Mr. Wimby. State senator. Presently running for the Big One.

Huh, folks? Hey! Sure could use your vote!"

"I don't think that's funny," whispered Jill. "I don't think politics is funny. It's deadly *serious.*"

"I know," he said. "I know."

"You know, your thesis—*Jeez Louise.*"

"I know—"

But the noise cut him off.

"Hey, no electioneering allowed," shouted out Ginger, setting forth another round of laughter. "I do pick them, don't I? But of course who *would* be here, after all, but people with professions. At how much a plate, Tommy?"

He smiled. "Enough, Gin. A nice place, huh? Gentlemen?"

"Best place in town," said the banker. "Anybody try the fried worms?"

"Indeed," said the federal court judge. "Anybody try the barnacles?"

"Out of my league," said Ginger. "Now . . . last, but surely not least!" she proclaimed, turning to a man in a very expensive looking black suit. It hung so well, Dean thought. It argued that appearances certainly did count.

"Mr. Keller," sang out the man. "Microchips! And let me set the record straight—the bird nests are the best choice! Hands down!"

"Is that right? Well . . . a Technical Man," exclaimed Ginger. "Well, how do, Mr. Science?"

"Just wonderful," said Mr. Keller. "This is . . . well, hell, it's making the evening quite interesting. And enjoyable."

"He hasn't seen *anything* yet," yelled Ginger, laughing. "But first! Time to mingle. A prerequisite to good form: Meet your Dance Partner. Don't go on a bunch of preconceived notions—oh, well, you get the picture!"

"We get it," shouted out Great Uncle George. "Step this way, Dancers, have a seat. Take a load off!"

"Ten minutes!" yelled Ginger. "And then Dance Time!"

And they began to take their Guest Dancers chairs at the long table as Great Uncle Tommy and Gere reclaimed their chairs. Mr.

Keller sat directly across from Great Uncle Tommy.

"Microchips," said Great Uncle Tommy. "Certainly the wave of the future."

"Oh, indeed, and since you're in weapons, Mr. Gumm—"

"Oh, hell, call me Tommy. That's what my friends call me."

"Tommy, then. My name's Will. Now since you're in weapons, let me point out that our new research—totally available to the public, as you've probably seen on the Internet, not divulging any secrets here—shows that these new chips can be strategically placed to kill the Enemy where he stands. Or sits! An internal battle—avoiding the external altogether. Just a matter of how to deliver the chips, and that's getting easier all the time: airborne, food-borne, water-borne, you name it. It's a whole new war scenario we're looking at, Tommy."

Sitting next to Will Keller was Mr. Dollar, the banker. "Of course I'm aware of that," he shouted out over the general buzz, "and the market is certainly growing, but how do you yourself rate it risk-wise?"

"Excellent, with market growth looking at about a half trillion come the next decade," said Will Keller.

"I've read that too," said Mr. Dollar.

At this point Mr. Wimby, the senator, leaned over from where he sat next to Mr. Dollar and said, "I wholeheartedly endorse whatever you can do to push legislation through to chip the criminals, the parolees, the mobsters, the Alzheimer's victims, the security risks, and infants for their own safety, dogs, cats, other pets, wild and tamed—because as a society, we've got too many weak links, at least as far as I'm concerned."

"Well, bravo!" sang out Mr. Keller. "You're absolutely right, and what you're addressing there represents a good portion of our market penetration. But new weapons concepts are our latest. And our most important future market. Now there's where"—he leaned forward to speak to Mr. Dollar—"your venture capital needs to be placed."

"I don't doubt it at all," said Mr. Dollar smiling.

"You'll run into some civil rights issues on that chipping," stated Mr. Armour, the federal court judge, seated next to Mr. Wimby. "We've already gotten into that a bit with some parolees. Weapons, though, that's a different matter, because it's the Enemy you're talking about there."

"The Wrong Side!" shouted Cousin Gere.

"That's a time, son!" rang out Uncle Rory.

"Oh, dear," rang out Aunt Winnie.

"Why does she always say that?" asked Dean's mother. But then she turned her attention to Jill again.

"She's such a . . . your mother!" whispered Jill.

"What are you whispering at my son?" snapped Dean's mother. "Don't you think I can see you?"

"I'm well aware," said Jill.

Great Aunt Sally seemed about to speak, and Dean noticed the vial of pills clutched in Great Uncle George's hand.

"Well, where were we?" asked Mr. Keller. "Oh. What I was about to say. We've got a saying in the weapons literature, which is also on the Internet—we didn't start it, but anyway we picked it up from whoever did: 'Chip Them, Clip Them.'"

"Ha! Ha!" roared Cousin Gere. "I like that! Only . . . will that mean no regular weapons anymore. No conventional—"

Great Uncle Tommy held up his hand. "There is *always* a need, and there will always *be* a need, for your external weapons, whether conventional or nuclear."

"Don't know about that," came back Mr. Keller, shaking his head. "It's a New Age, Tommy. Don't know about that—give it fifty years. See what you say then."

"I won't be around to say!" said Great Uncle Tommy.

"Yeah, we'll all be dead and gone," said Mr. Keller, and laughed. Then he grimaced.

"You can bet on one thing, though," said Mr. Armour. "There'll be litigation over it. There's litigation over practically everything in this world—if you think about it. Rights, rights, rights. Public versus private. Civil rights, private rights, fetal rights, animal rights, vermin rights! ...I could go on. But let's look at it this way, and I'm not popular in some circles for saying this: Criminals *have* no rights. Are you there with me? Everybody there with me? They *have* no rights."

"I'm with you on that," said Mr. Keller.

"I'm certainly with you," said Great Uncle Tommy. "They've given up whatever rights they had. Once they crossed that line."

"Shoot and ask questions later," said Gere. And he gave a thumbs up.

"Depends on the criminal," said Senator Wimby. "Doesn't it?"

"What do you mean?" asked Mr. Armour.

"You getting this for your thesis?" asked Great Uncle Tommy, nudging Dean.

"What? I don't see—"

"*Criminals*—huh? And the straight dope from *real* Officials here—huh? War Criminals?"

Dean heard the capitalizations, but before he could respond, Ginger was hailing them. And tinging a spoon against a cup. "Time! Time! Time! Hurry up—please."

Quiet followed. A hush.

"Jen?"

Jen jumped in. "Now," said Jen, at the mic, "it's time to line up again—oh, ye Dancers! Behold, please do assemble!"

Dean noticed that people at other tables were looking their way, turning their seats toward them—to get a better look. It was about to happen. They were about to see the Dance Team swing into action. The dance floor began to clear, the dancers gliding off the polished sheen of the hardwood toward the many tables, seeking their seating.

The men began to head out from the table to the floor, and there were laughs and applause by Uncle Rory and Great Uncle George, and squeals of laughter from Aunt Winnie and Dean's mother. But Dean inched forward and saw that Great Aunt Sally was silently looking off in space at the dance floor, or perhaps at the other people at the many tables.

When they were once again all lined up, Ginger again whispered in Cousin Gere's ear. He nodded, grimaced, and then smirked.

Now Jen sang out: "I already see pretty darned good posture here, so our time being limited, we'll spend it on smiling—my ole forte. It's time to perfect those smiles—to make them just per-*feect*. Get hold of those smile lines and make them work for you. You, sir, Mr. Dollar, are a banker. How important is a smile in your profession?"

"Very important," said Dollar. "Exceedingly."

"And you, Mr. Wimby, how important is a smile in your area?"

"More important than in his!" shouted out Wimby. "Or *his*"— and he pointed at the Federal Court judge, Mr. Armour.

All the men laughed, and Dean watched roars of laughter coming from Uncle Rory and Great Uncle George. They sounded like snorts.

"Good, good, good!" laughed Jennifer gleefully.

"Better damn well smile," said Cousin Gere. "Or you'll never get through it."

And suddenly Great Uncle George rose and sang out, in a rich alto, the first lyrics of the smile song from Chaplin's *Modern Times*, and Dean felt tears welling up. He'd always wept at that song, or was it Great Uncle George's haunting voice?

He wiped each eye. "What's wrong?" asked Jill.

"Nothing," he said.

"You're a tender little soul, aren't you?" she said.

"Smile, smile, smile!" rang out Jennifer. "And you all, I'll just bet, already know how to smile, so you probably don't need my help at all. But I'm going to, humble little me that I am, I'm going to see if I can more nearly per*fect* that smile—are we agreed?"

"Yes, ma'am," Mr. Dollar, the banker, yelled out, and laughed, and the others joined in.

"I'll smile all right," said Gere, but Dean saw nothing but disdain in that smirk.

"All in good fun, son," Uncle Rory yelled. "All in good fun."

And the next ten minutes, Dean timed it, fearing that Jill would suddenly take off, were spent with Jennifer giving the men pointers on Better Smiling. "Show yourself Confident," she said. "That's what a smile shows: You're Confident. You believe in What You Are. You're Assertive!"

Dean watched as Jennifer actually helped form each Dancer's smile, tightening the smile lines, or loosening them just so. Now and then she'd turn to the audience at the table and explain what she was doing, like the professional trainer she was, and Dean looked and saw Aunt Winnie actually trying it out on her own face. When Jennifer got to Cousin Gere, she stretched his cheeks like a rubber mask—to get, Dean figured, that tendency to sneer off his face.

"I *do* have to get home," spoke up Jill. "I really think this is over the top, and if I don't have my paper in order by Monday, I'm just dead meat, I tell you."

"Yes," he said. "Yes."

But he didn't budge.

"Well?" she said.

"Soon," he said.

She sighed. "Might as well enjoy it, huh?"

And then Ginger suddenly escorted Cousin Gere to the mic. Static. Bad static. And then she shouted out: "And now, notice. Oh, do notice. You see who's beside me? This is Sergeant Gere Packall, brave Marine in his uniform, with his many medals. You will hear from this Marine before the Dance begins. You will hear now!"

A round of clapping. Clapping, oohing, aahing, filling the entire Soft-Shoe.

Gere took to the mic. He waited. He waited until the clapping began to subside. He waited. Dean could see him only from the back, that powerful, brutal body of his.

"I come to you," said Gere. "Here tonight. With only a few words. Okay, chief, if you don't support the war, you are an f-ing coward! You got it?"

Ginger leaned toward him. She whispered. She was shaking her head.

"Yeah, yeah," said Gere. "Yeah, yeah. You better put your goddamned money where your mouth is, is all I can say. You live it, chief, like I do. War, war, war. It don't get better than that. No, ace.

Kill those goddamned fuckers where they stand. Or sit. Huh? You bet, slick!"

Gere backed away from the mic.

At first, there wasn't any clapping. But then it began and it was like a storm when it hit. It went on and on and on, and Dean didn't think it would stop. But finally it began to subside, and then it eventually quit, and Ginger escorted Gere toward the mic and shouted, "Here is one brave Marine!"

More clapping, and then in a half minute or so, it was over. Gere was returning to his fellow Dancers.

Dean waited.

"Is he even human?" said Jill. "Is he even animal?"

"Don't know," said Dean. "I wish."

"What?"

"Nothing."

"Whoever sired him," said Jill.

Dean glanced at Uncle Rory and Aunt Winnie. But their eyes were on Gere as best as he could tell.

And then the festivities finally did begin—suddenly. The group of six men, now lined up like Greek dancers, striking poses, sensing that this was *it*—now, yes, they were on stage, about to perform.

Dean saw the crowds at the tables knowing this, knowing it was coming. But Ginger was now turned toward *their* table, toward the reunion group. As were the Dancers.

"I give you!" shouted Ginger, grabbing the mic, "our Dance Team for the Big One!—to be center stage for the Fundraising Festivities for the Troops: not in order of importance, nay, but in order of placement—yes, here they *are*: Mr. Gumm, Weapons Manufacturer; Mr. Packall, Brave Military Man in his Marine Uniform; Mr. Dollar, Banker; Mr. Armour, Federal Court Judge; Mr. Wimby, Senator; and last, but certainly not least, Mr. Keller, Microchip Man—all itching to Dance and Prance! Ginger made a hushing noise. "Now, now, folks, we need a drum roll. We need us a big, big drum roll . . ."

And Dean watched as Great Uncle George began to do it. And Uncle Rory let loose as a backup. And then he turned to Jill, and she was shaking her head, back and forth, back and forth. She had her mouth against his ear. "Abominable. Aesthetically disgusting." He nodded. His mother was smiling, starting to laugh. Aunt Sally had her face in her hands. She looked up, looked down, put her face in her hands. Tired, maybe. Bored maybe. Didn't think this was all that much fun. Wanted to go to bed.

"Dance and Prance!" shouted out Ginger. "You know how! Do what comes natural!"

Music burst forth from the band, flooding the Soft-Shoe.

And then, almost at once, the Dance Team began to dance—still facing the reunion table. *They* were getting the premier performance—they! The Dancers cavorting, doing the soft-shoe, the tap dance, about anything, apparently that came to mind. Then: Great Uncle Tommy doing a kind of high step, coming down hard on the floor with each leap, like he was Peter Pan—and that same easeful smile; then the banker, Mr. Dollar, joining in with smooth jumps and turns, all the while watching his own posture in his handsome suit, and smiling brightly; and then, yes, even Cousin Gere, jogging in place, patting the medals on his chest, a look of vanity and outrage, but it passed soon, and went to a smirk; and then Mr. Armour, the judge, twirling around, looking behind his back, twirling, as though he didn't know which direction to go—was that a dance step? And then Mr. Wimby, joyfully waltzing about, as though he were on the Yellow Brick Road in *The Wizard of Oz*. And finally, Mr. Keller, stomping, kicking, stomping, then attempting to glide over the floor. And the whole table howling with snorts, guffaws, and peals of giddy laughter.

"Horrid," whispered Jill. "Just horrid. Obscene!"

But this was not all—Ginger whirling her hand above her head, shouting out at the mic to the audience at large: "I give you the Jen and Gin Dance Team Show!"

Loud applause from the audience at large. But yells too: "Turn this way! Hey! *This* way!" And: "Don't be bashful! Come on now!"

Now all six Dancers, each and every one of the six men, huddled and then burst forth into position, beginning a synchronized soft-shoe, suddenly turning their backs to the reunion table and facing the wide sea of tables. Dean was unable not to look, unable not to study each movement of each shiny shoe as the six men danced away. And the music changed, so that it was wonderfully appropriate to this soft-shoe, and the men moved in unison, their hands in the air, like tamed savages, as the applause rained on them from everywhere, a chain-effect, from table to table, of clapping, the audience at the tables rising from their seats, like at a curtain call. It was as though the six Dancers assembled before them represented something very important, on the order of an epiphany. Registering now. This was it. A spectacle, but something on the order of the sacred.

And then Dean looked down the table at Great Aunt Sally, and what had struck him for just a second—a vagrant thought of *uh, oh*—proved to be absolutely true: there, holding her face in her hands, was Great Aunt Sally, sobbing, and Great Uncle George close by with that vial of pills, attempting to dispense one as before.

And then she suddenly rose from her chair. She went vertical.

He watched, listened. Was she going to join the Dancers? No, he didn't believe it. He didn't believe that for a second.

She suddenly cupped her mouth, like a megaphone. "I've seen it," she cried. "I've seen it!"

But she was drowned out. Static.

"I give you," shouted the man at the mic. "The Jen and Gin Dance Team!"

"Sal!" Great Uncle George yelled. "Sit down!"

"First death!" shouted Aunt Sally, megaphoning it. A plaintive cry, it was, with a shriek.

"Sit, sit, sit!" hushed Great Uncle George.

But she still stood. "Then the judgment!"

"*Sit.*"

And she sat down.

Great Uncle George sat down.

"I give you," shouted the man at the mic, even louder. "The Jen and Gin Dance Team!"

The Dance Team now began prancing toward the center of the dance floor. Their steps were a combo of smooth, unctuous moves and harsh thrusts, like jackhammers.

Dean watched it.

He studied it.

Something in him begin to surface. He felt himself rising.

Jill grabbed him. "Hey! You leaving?"

"Got something to do," he said.

"What?"

"Something . . . must . . . I must."

He was being pulled away from his chair. Something had grabbed hold, fist-like, of his very soul. He felt it in his legs, something hurrying them along, as fast as the legs of those Dancers from the other tables had frolicked over to the reunion table, with Jennifer and Ginger leading them. He turned for just a second and saw Jill, one finger pressed against her supple red lips, eyeing him. She looked about to speak. Was shock the right word? Yes, he knew it was. Nonetheless, Dean was now frisking toward Ginger, whose back was toward him, and toward Jennifer, the two of them clap clapping hard at the Dance Team as they once again began to dance, jive, cavort, and explode into action.

The Dance Team was moving frenetically to a new beat, a bouncy brazen beat by the band, now utterly raucous. It sounded somehow like a mix of cowboy, gospel, and martial cadences, with tinges of mournful wails from a sax that called to mind a saloon thick with booze, cigarette smoke, and strip tease acts. The sound of the Dancers on the floor made him think of the hooves of buffalos, about to be slaughtered on the prairie. But he corrected this vagrant thought—nobody would be massacring this Dance Team. Look at that spellbound crowd, still standing, still shouting out electrified words of praise.

The two women, almost simultaneously, caught Dean's look as he burst onto the dance floor. They exchanged momentary glances with each other, then with him. Something peremptory about Ginger's: something untoward about to happen? This was not according to the Official Dance Team Fundraising Festivities, Dean supposed, but he nonetheless moved on.

The Dance Team suddenly spun from a line into a circle. Their steps fierce now, morbid even, macabre.

He watched, heard, *felt* the Dancers, as he approached them. He felt pulled in by the circle of heavy clomps, into its whirling vortex. His gut sank as they seemed to suck up every ounce of his being through the pounding of their feet on the hard floor, their jiving bodies, their flailing arms, bobbing heads, the thunderous cacophony of music that felt as though it were about to do serious damage to the structure of the building, the resounding applause from the crowd. But he would be bold: he continued to make his way out, foot by foot now, to the middle of the dance floor, like a man, he thought, creeping about, unauthorized onto a gym floor—no gym shoes, sporting civilian clothes. After all, he was not about to find a dance partner; he was not about to dance. He was about to speak—he was about to pitch his question. It was time, indeed, to pitch his question for as many ears as possible to hear. It was heaving in his chest, it was heaving in his soul, and required relief in utterance.

He was now on stage—this was *his* moment. He panned the Soft-Shoe's crowd, the vast sea of faces, jubilant, rollicking with hilarity, expectant, quizzical, stunned; the many hands waving at him, hands and fists swinging, whirling above heads; the many shouts directed now at *him*, a mix of the vile, the venomous, and the zealously supportive: for here, some surely took it, was a man who would direct the dance steps of the Dancers—or here perhaps was a man who would lead a new dance step. This was good or bad, depending on your point of view.

He was confused on how to proceed. But in that confusion, Dean suddenly gained clarity. He could not stop or soften the music, but he could at least thunder out above it. He heard himself shouting out words that were not at first clear even to *him*: words that were confused, lacking all rationality—more like visceral bellyings and brayings forth, inane guttural pronouncements about nothing at all, or at least nothing that made a lick of sense. Confirming his worst fears. Raw notes. A very early rough draft. And such static: the now screeching and squawking band, the maniacal footwork of the Dancers, the crowd's numberless faces, waving hands, shouts, boos, hisses, guffaws, raucous snorts—he looked to find himself. Where *was* he? He waved away the buzz of everything around him—this storm of locusts causing great obfuscation. He would now speak the actual message, that which he'd been wanting to say for so long—and to so many people, all here, all captive now. This was indeed the product of daydream, fantasy, the veritable wish list.

"Why the bombing," cried out Dean, "the stabbing, the shooting, the blowing up, the burning, the flaying alive, the burying. The bodies torn and broken. Why that?" This was clearer now, but surely still the pleas of a madman. He went on, ignored the upheaval of rank laughter and movement from the crowd, in an effort to be more rational—yes, of a certain—and with unequivocal gravitas. And especially, he thought, grimly, with such a bevy of riotous detractors out there, grinning, sneering, making inappropriate finger gestures, bent on pricking his bubble. He bellied forth: "You, and you, and you, and *you*!" he sang out. "You tell me why!" He started to go on, but despaired. How continue? How sound halfway intelligent? How sound hallway sane? "Why?" he yelled. 'Why is it?" He felt his face grow hot, his stomach sicken, his legs go weak. "Why?" he cried.

The Dance Team beat the floor harder than ever. And now he felt stifled by their shouts, hurrahs, and gleeful crescendos, but he didn't look. He was still facing the huge crowd—but mute now, mesmerized, blank of thought.

Suddenly, a well-dressed man in a tan suit stood up, yelled out: "Hey, Professor, is this going to be on the test?"

Dean tried to answer.

Another: "Call the Straight Jacket Men!"

Dean quivered.

And then someone shouted out, but where from?—a big, brassy shout, lubricated with hard drinks, drowning out the shouts and the pounding foot beats of the Dance Team—"*They're* insane enough, buddy! Dance or get off the goddamned floor!"

A thunderous clapping, followed by a shout, which soon became contagious: "Take a bow! Take a bow!" Fists, fingers, gyrating hands signaling him on.

Dean stood, paralyzed, on the dance floor.

He saw the white curtains billowing against the walls, and they seemed like ghostly presences beckoning him on. "All the war dead!" he cried out. "All of them! Bloody fields—spears, swords, axes, artillery, bombs, guns, grenades—"

"Don't be a goddamned coward, Howard!" some guy with a thick beard yelled out.

He pondered it all, on the periphery of the centrifugal force of the Dance Team, boisterously wheeling about, six men circling, creating palpable, seductive energy.

Their busy shiny shoes, their jacked-up smirks, their twisted, contorted lips. He felt sick to stand here and behold them, sick deep in his soul—sick at what he was seeing. He must not look, yet he could not *but* look, as the Dance Team still spun away, bright faces made even brighter in the incredible sheen of the dance floor.

The band roared on.

But was he seeing correctly? Was that Great Aunt Sally at the mic? Was that her voice, plaintive, raspy? "First death," she rang out. "Then the judgment! Yes, oh, dear, yes! The judgment!" And Great Uncle George standing there, coaxing with that vial. But the woman was glued to the mic. Weeping, weeping, and then a sudden shout, one he wouldn't have imagined: "Death, death, death!" Stronger. Stronger. Such energy, such force!

My god, the woman had grown fierce, her face dark with blood wonder. Even from here he could see her trembling lips, those white eyes harsh with indisputable invective. Directed right at the dancers, right at those shiny shoes, right at those shiny smirks. He tried to catch her eye, but her gaze was unwavering.

About the Author

Jack Smith's satirical novel *Hog to Hog* won the 2007 George Garrett Fiction Prize and was published by Texas Review Press in 2008. His novel *Icon* was published by Serving House Books in 2014. His novel *Being* was also published by Serving House Books, in 2015. He has published stories in a number of literary magazines, including *Southern Review, North American Review, Texas Review, X-Connect, In Posse Review,* and *Night Train.* His reviews have appeared widely in such publications as *Ploughshares, Georgia Review, American Book Review, Prairie Schooner, Mid-American Review, Pleiades, The Missouri Review,* and *Environment* magazine. He has published a few dozen articles in both *Novel & Short Story Writer's Market* and *The Writer* magazine. His creative writing book, *Write and Revise for Publication: A 6-Month Plan for Crafting an Exceptional Novel and Other Works of Fiction,* was published in 2013 by Writer's Digest Books. His coauthored nonfiction environmental book entitled *Killing Me Softly* was published by Monthly Review Press in 2002. Besides his writing, Smith was fiction editor of *The Green Hills Literary Lantern,* an online literary magazine published by Truman State University, for 25 years.

www.ingramcontent.com/pod-product-compliance
Lightning Source LLC
Chambersburg PA
CBHW031851170626
46807CB00004B/1666